"Russt," I say, tucking my iPod into my bag so he won't see that I'm listening to the Walters.

He sits down on the edge of my blanket by my outstretched feet. As if he's welcome. I remember that Penny told me that Russ is on campus most days, finishing up some paper for a class, which he didn't turn in on time last semester—he needs it to become a senior next year.

"Haven't seen you around this week," he says. "You been working hard at Amalgam?"

"Yeah," I say. "It keeps me busy."

"So busy you can't even come next door to hang out?" he asks, leaning up on one arm and looking at me sideways.

"I've had my own stuff going on," I say.

In the mottled sunlight through the trees, he looks like an old movie star, someone out of a Western who belongs on a horse with a gun slung around his waist. But here he is, on my blanket in the shade. And when he's not being obnoxious, he's kind of . . .

MELISSA WALKER

Lovestruck Summer

HARPER TEEN

An Imprint of HarperCollins*Publishers*

HarperTeen is an imprint
of HarperCollins Publishers.

Library of Congress catalog card number:
2008931134
ISBN 978-0-06-171586-0

Typography by Andrea Vandergrift
09 10 11 12 13 OPM 10 9 8 7 6 5 4 3 2 1
❖
First Edition

Thanks to my grandparents, Don and Priscilla "Tay" Day, who taught me to love "old" music and danced like a dream. And to my blog readers on www.melissacwalker.com, who thought of the Best. Band. Names. Ever. You guys rock.

Chapter 1

$\mathcal{I}$ live my life in headphones. That way, I can control what I let in. If kids at school are being idiotic and perky, I put on a mellow track and tune out their spirit rally. If my parents are nagging me, I play a fast song and rock out in my mind while smiling and nodding at them.

That's what I'm doing right now, at our dinner table. Mom and Dad gave up the "no headphones" fight last year when I proved I could listen to music and to them at the same time. The truth is, I can't really do that, but they repeat themselves so much and their body language is so transparent that I always know what they're saying, or at least the gist of it. Like I can see that Dad is using his fork for emphasis as he lays down rules for the summer, and Mom is pursing her lips and smiling, which she does when she's trying to punctuate a point that Dad's making.

I just graduated from high school, like, last week. I tweaked my cap and gown by adding red silk swatches that streamed down the sides, and my best friend, Raina, and I celebrated by ditching all the stupid graduation parties and driving to Carolina Beach to listen to the new Walters album. They're my favorite band, and their label, Amalgam Records, is in Austin, Texas—a place I've always wanted to see. We listened to all four Walters albums in succession on my iPod. Not on shuffle either—but in the song order the band intended. And it gave me and Raina a brilliant idea.

"What's the number for Amalgam Records?" I asked.

Raina grabbed her BlackBerry. Ten seconds later, she rattled off the digits. It was three A.M., but someone actually answered, and I actually played it cool.

"Amalgam."

"Hi, this is Quinn Parker," I said, using my adult voice. "I'd like to inquire about an internship with your company. I'm well-versed in your bands, and I'm willing to do anything you need—filing, mailing, getting coffee. Are internships available this summer?"

Silence on the other end.

Then, in a burst of silliness, I shouted, "Say yes!"

"Sure," said the guy on the other end, who was starting to sound cute to me after two words. "Did you want to start next week?"

"Um, how about the week of June twentieth?" I said, gesturing wildly at Raina. *This is working!*

"Cool," said cute indie boy, who I had decided was my soon-to-be-boyfriend. "I'm Rick. Ask for me when you get here."

Then he was gone. And I was psyched.

So that's how I fully took control of my destiny and set up my first summer away from home. My parents are both professors at the university in our town, and they're going on a research trip to Ecuador for July and August. They expected me to stay home and water the plants, I think, but I convinced them that it would be better if I went to Austin for this "career opportunity."

Of course, I told them I'd had to go through all sorts of trouble to apply—sending grades, recommendations, a personal essay—since it's such a coveted music internship. They liked the sound of that. Mom and Dad are big on "life experience" résumé boosters.

Besides, I'm heading to college in the fall—the University of Vermont—so if I stay home in North Carolina, the summer would be one long farewell with Raina while I work my job at the local movie theater. It would just be *the same*. So Texas it is.

At the dinner table tonight, my parents are going through the Austin Rules, which include: "No Drinking, No Boy Sleepovers, and Listen to Penny."

Penny, my cousin, is a junior at The University of Texas in Austin, and she lives in a condo down there, which my aunt and uncle bought for her when she went away to college. I'm not saying she's spoiled, but . . . you do the math. My parents L-O-V-E her because she's following in their footsteps and studying International Politics so she can be a professor just like they are. I haven't seen her in a while, but the last time she visited she had just finished her fresh-man year, and she went on and on about how she spends *hours* in the library studying—even during the summer. In other words, she is the perfect person for me to live with. She'll never be around to keep tabs on me. And let's just say that since Austin is the live-music capital of the world and I am going to be a valued intern at one of the coolest independent music labels in the country, I might have some late nights.

I pull off my headphones as a sign of respect because I can tell that Mom and Dad are near-ing the end of the Rules talk.

". . . and Priscilla, remember to call us at least once a week," finishes Mom.

Did I not mention that my real name is Priscilla? I go by Quinn, my middle name, because . . . well . . . it's obvious. Priscilla is a frilly old lady with heirloom jewelry and silk scarves and a dyed-blond beehive. I am an eighteen-year-old hipster in jeans and soft tees, who uses multiple dyes to get just the right shade of messed-up blue in my blunt boy-length hair, which, if I left it alone, would be naturally blond. But who wants that? Only my mom gets away with "Priscilla" because it was my grandmother's name and she died before I was born, so I get why it's important. But to the rest of the world, it's Quinn.

"I will, Mom," I say, smiling and batting my brown eyes to show her what a great daughter I am.

"And don't fall in love," adds Dad, picking up his plate to carry it into the kitchen. "Those Texas boys are trouble."

"Don't worry," I say.

I avoid telling my dad that I already have a pseudo crush on whoever answered the phone at Amalgam Records, and that my real summer goal—besides listening to tons of live music and enjoying life without parental supervision—is to snag the perfect indie-music-loving boyfriend. Raina is calling him "The Supreme" because she has to have a title for everything. All through high school, I've been longing for a boyfriend who could appreciate the poetry of the Pixies instead of the latest radio countdown hit, but my school is full of future frat boys. My Austin guy will be so different.

I can already picture him—piecey dark hair,

sharp-angled glasses, intense eyes, and lips that part slightly in awed admiration as he watches his favorite bands onstage. He'll be able to recite all the Walters lyrics by heart, he'll wear Converse sneakers (unless we're dressing up, in which case he might wear Campers), and he may even be an early Weezer fan who still reads Rivers Cuomo's blog. Who knows?

What I do know is that he is in Austin, and I cannot wait for my summer to start.

Chapter 2

When Penny picks me up at the airport, I'm shocked.

It's not just one thing, although if I were splitting hairs I might mention my cousin's perfectly blown-out dark brown locks or her shiny, possibly newly whitened smile, or the extra-large logo-covered Louis Vuitton purse she's holding. But really, it's the big picture that overwhelms me: Penny has gone Texas.

She screams as she runs up to hug me at baggage claim, knocking my arm with her giant pocketbook, and leaving a bright mark on my cheek with her impossibly red lipstick.

"Hey!" she says, taking a step back to look at me. "Quinn, you are such a little alterna-girl right now."

I cringe. I know she's just saying that

because my hair is dyed. Or maybe it's because I'm just wearing Tom's of Maine deodorant and not a hundred sprays of the latest floral scent from Macy's. I smile at my cousin and resist the urge to wave her perfume cloud away.

"Hey," I say with less twang and more nonchalance than she has.

"We are gonna have so much fun this summer!" Penny squeals, reaching into her purse for her car keys. I notice the BMW key chain and follow her cautiously as her yellow kitten heels *click-click* on the cold airport floor.

When the doors open to the parking deck, something almost knocks me down.

"Good Lord!" I shout, dropping my giant duffel bag in protest. "It is freaking *hot* out here!" The air around me feels almost solid, and I immediately start to sweat. Penny, however, is clip-clopping her way to the car without a pause.

"Keep up, Quinny!" she singsong shouts. "It's only June. Wait till August." Then she flashes me a blinding smile and puts her key into the trunk of a bright red BMW.

"Graduation present," she purrs, noticing

that my eyes are widening.

"You're a junior," I say.

"Rising senior," she corrects. "And Dad knows I did really well this semester."

Is this really the Penny who spends all her time in the library? I think as I load my heavy bag into the trunk. I guess it's been a couple of years since I've seen her, but still.

I slide into the front—pale leather—seat as she raises one bubble-gum-pink manicured hand to press the button that opens the sunroof. When she starts the car, my ears are flooded with a hip-hop ballad that, while undeniably catchy, is also intolerable. She cranks it up and starts to sing. And I start to worry. Can I survive a whole summer with this girl?

By the time we get to Penny's condo, I realize that my cousin really is not who I thought she was. Yes, she's majoring in International Politics, and yes, she's related to me. That hasn't changed. The new factoids I've discovered are disturbing to say the least. For example: 1) Penny spends no less than one hour in the bathroom each morning, blowing out her shiny mane of movie-star hair.

2) Penny sleeps in her bra so her boobs won't sag. 3) Penny also sleeps in her teeth-whitening strips, although her dentist told her not to and her teeth sometimes tingle painfully. 4) Penny is contemplating a boob job, but one of her "sisters" just had a scary anesthesia episode, so she might hold off for now. And, oh yeah, number one most horrifying revelation on the car ride: 5) Penny is the newly elected president of a powerful University of Texas sorority—the UT Tri-Pis.

I half thought she was kidding about the sorority thing, but when we walk into the condo, I realize that she is dead serious. Above the faux-marble mantle, there are metallic purple letters that say PI PI PI. Atop every surface in the living room—from end tables to window-sills—are framed photos showcasing the elec-tric smiles of groups of girls in rainbow-colored dresses with cookie-cutter guys at their sides. Each one marks an idiotically named event: MAY 5TH BOOZE CRUISE!, DECEMBER 4TH HOLIDAY HOEDOWN, OCTOBER 28TH PUMPKIN PROMENADE. And on the coffee table, I spy a book called *Rules for Rush*. There is a TOP SECRET stamp across the cover. Somehow I don't think it's ironic.

I drop my duffel bag on the ivory carpet and sit down, fighting a pang of panic. I will my mind to search for things that are positive, things that are right about the situation I'm in. I look around quickly and mentally note three: 1) The AC in here is way good. It's, like, sixty-five degrees. 2) I see a huge bowl of fruit through the kitchen door, so I know Penny grocery shops and isn't a huge fast-food junkie like lots of college students I've heard about. 3) This couch is pretty comfortable.

Okay, I'm calmer.

"It's great here," I say, grinning up at Penny with what I hope is a winning expression.

"Thanks!" says Penny, kicking off her shoes and joining me on the couch.

"This is really soft," I say, patting the pastel blue cushion underneath me.

"I know," says Penny. "I knew you wouldn't mind sleeping on it! My friend Chrissy said you'd be annoyed, but I told her it was a really plush couch."

Hold the phone. "I thought this was a two-bedroom," I say in my just-wondering-not-getting-aggressive voice.

"It is," says Penny, glancing upstairs. "But Miss Tiara is so used to sleeping in the second room that we can't really upset her routine."

I follow Penny's eyes. Is there a beauty queen roommate too?

"Miss Tiara?" I ask.

"I'll bring her down!" says Penny, standing and bounding upstairs. She comes back down twenty seconds later with a fluffy white dog in her arms.

"She's a little precious doll, yes, she is," Penny is baby-talking to the fluffball. "Miss Tiara, meet Quinn!" She makes the fake-looking dog fake-wave to me. I plaster a smile on my face.

"Does Miss Tiara wanna give Quinny a tour?" asks Penny, still baby-talking. Then she answers her own question: "Yes, she does! She sure does!"

I guess that's my cue to stand up and follow my sorority-girl cousin and her room-stealing dog around the condo. After we've baby-talked through the kitchen, which has a marbled pink backsplash behind the stove, we check out the downstairs half bath, which will be my main port of call as resident couch-sleeper. At least the mirror opens up to a space large enough to hold my deodorant and floss, I note.

We head upstairs, and after seeing the Pepto-Bismol tidal wave of a room that Penny sleeps in, I'm a little scared as she opens the door to Miss Tiara's abode. There are more purple metallic letters—this time they simply say MT, and they hang on the blissfully white far wall. In the center of the room, there sits a large, lacy pillow surrounded by picture frames with photos of Miss Tiara in various states of accessorizing—sun hat at the beach, pearls for a formal event, even tiny glasses for what must have been a studious day.

"It's not fully decorated," says Penny-the-obvious. I realize my jaw is a little open and I shut it.

"Cool," I say, because, I mean, what am I supposed to say? Should I voice my objection to the fact that the dog has a room to herself with one pillow in the center of a small shrine while I am relegated to the completely un-private living room downstairs? I guess that might be rude when Penny's taking me in rent free. In the condo that her parents, my aunt and uncle, bought for her. And one that she probably doesn't have to pay for at all anyway.

Oops, was that a negative rant I just went on? I'm working on that.

"We three are going to be just like sisters here!" Penny giggles. "Well, sisters and a brother."

Please don't tell me there's a frat boy in the closet. "Brother?" I ask.

"Oh, Miss Tiara's a boy," whispers Penny, covering the dog's ears. "He just likes to be in drag, and he prefers to be referred to as 'she.' There's a really cool cross-dresser named Leslie who walks around town, and Miss Tiara has just taken to him as a role model."

I laugh. It's the first thing my cousin's said all day that's weird in a good way.

"Want some fruit?" asks Penny.

I nod as she puts down Miss Tiara and we head downstairs. I look at the couch—my bed—as we pass through the living room. It *is* pretty plush. And I notice that there's a cord on the stereo next to the TV, where I can plug in my iPod and listen to music. There's even a sliding glass door past the kitchen that leads out to the deck in the back, which looks like a nice spot to hang out.

"Honeybell orange?" asks Penny when we get to the kitchen. She's holding out a bulbous citrus fruit. "They're a cross between tangerines and ruby red grapefruit."

We settle onto two barstools and share our first Austin snack.

Chapter 3

By early evening, I have my "bed" all set up and my duffel bag unpacked. Penny cleared a drawer for me in a chest that sits in the living room, and I took over a shelf in the small storage closet under the stairs. My cousin also made space in Miss Tiara's closet for any dresses I brought. When I told her all I had were T-shirts, jeans, and one jean skirt in case we went out to a nice dinner sometime, she gasped. Then she immediately got out some fabric scissors and insisted that I make at least one of my four pairs of jeans into cutoffs.

I protested, but she grabbed me by the sleeve and marched me over to the deck door, sliding it open and gesturing wildly with her pink nails. "Quinn! It is just too hot out there for you to be running around in full-leg pants!"

After a blast of heat, I had to agree. But when she tried to BeDazzle the hems of my new cut-offs with pink-and-purple rhinestones, I put my foot down.

There's a large, overstuffed chair in the corner of the living room right next to the stereo. It's pink with yellow flowers on it, and it's a little fussy, but it has a great footrest. After I finish unpacking, I settle into it with my iPod and listen to the Walters.

As I'm drifting off into a state of music-induced bliss, I feel a rapid vibration and open my eyes to see Penny rushing down the stairs in a blur of pastel. She opens the front door and there's a blond girl in a Tri-Pi T-shirt, the purple letters stretched over her ginormous boobs. I briefly wonder if this is the recently surgeried friend, and then I see a guy standing behind her.

He has curly reddish-brown hair and he's actually wearing a checked shirt that's tucked into his jeans with a big belt buckle. I smirk. This guy is like a walking cowboy poster. I glance down at his feet and am surprised that he's wearing Converse and not spur-studded boots.

He and Penny are saying hello, and then he turns to face me just as the song on my iPod changes to my favorite slow track. It's the one that I want to be "our song." Well, not mine and this cowboy guy's, of course, although as he walks over to me, his smile grows and I spot two dimples on the sides of his tanned cheeks. He looks incredibly tall from this angle . . . and there's one curl that hangs in the middle of his forehead . . . and, *wow*, can anyone's eyes really be that blue?

"Quinn!" I hear Penny shouting through my musical haze. "Quinn!"

I press STOP and stand up, realizing that I've just been staring at Mr. Cowboy while he's been trying to shake my hand. I stumble over the footrest but try to play it off as I reach out for what I'm sure is going to be a brutish shake.

"I'm Quinn," I say.

"Call me Russ," he says, taking my hand gently and kissing it.

Whoa. Do people really do that outside of the movies? Weird.

He looks over at Penny. "I thought you told me her name was Priscilla," he says.

I glare at my cousin. She knows how much I don't like that name.

"She goes by Quinn," says Penny, ignoring my death stare.

"Pleasure to meet you, Priscilla," says Russ, grinning back at me.

I've known the guy five seconds and he's already trying to annoy me—and succeeding. He may be cute, but that doesn't mean I need to humor him. I give him a tight-lipped smile.

"I'm Chrissy," says boob-girl, rushing over and giving me a fierce hug.

I must look taken aback, because then she says, "I'm a hugger! But I know some people aren't. Sorry—did I just totally weird you out?"

"No," I lie. "It's okay."

"Quinn is an indie-rock girl," says Penny, like that inane label explains something about why I might shirk a stranger's hug.

"Oh, what are you listening to?" asks Russ, reaching down for my iPod.

I snatch it up before he can get it. "My favorite band," I say. "They're called the Walters, but I doubt you'd know them."

"They're from Austin," says Russ. "Of course I know them!"

Oh, right. Well, just because they're local doesn't mean he really listens to them.

"Let me guess," continues Russ, "your favorite album is *Look for It.*"

I blanch a little. He's right.

Russ laughs. "It's okay—when I was your age that was my favorite one too."

"I'm eighteen," I say, annoyed.

"That was my guess," he says.

"Well, how old are you?" I ask. He can't be more than nineteen.

"I'm twenty," he says. "And there's a big difference, Miss Priscilla."

"Don't antagonize my cousin!" shouts Penny.

Miss Tiara bounds down the stairs to join us.

"Mr. T!" shouts Russ. "What's up, man?"

"Russ, I've told you she likes to be called Miss Tiara," hisses Penny.

"I'm sorry, PP, but that dog is a boy, and I know you're committed to torturing him with necklaces and frilly dresses, but I'm not going

21

to participate." Russ winks at me.

"PP?" I ask, not sure I want to know.

"Party Penny!" shouts Chrissy. "It's Penny's nickname. And now since she's Tri-Pi President, we might call her PPP!"

"Why not just make it PPPPPP for Pi Pi Pi President Party Penny?" I ask with a slight sneer.

"That's kind of a mouthful," says Chrissy, not catching my sarcasm.

I look over at Russ and he's gazing at me intently, like he's trying to figure out something about me. It's a little disquieting.

"I'm starving," says Penny. "Quinn, we're taking you out to dinner."

"What kind of food do you like?" asks Chrissy, barreling ahead before I can answer her question. "Let's go to Shady Grove. Hopefully we can get an outdoor table. Do you maybe wanna change out of your jeans? You might get hot. It's cooler at night, but I still think you'd be more comfortable in a skirt or —"

"I'm fine," I say, wondering how I'm ever going to make it through dinner with Miss Tri-Pi

Chatterbox and Russ the wannabe cowboy.

"Are you sure?" Chrissy asks. "Because I could loan you a sundress or something. I've got a bunch next door."

"Oh, you live next door?" I ask.

"We both do," says Russ. "We share the condo to the left of Penny's as you walk out the door. Which means our walls touch yours."

Is he *trying* to be weird?

"Uh . . . cool," I say.

"They've been roommates forever but they haven't hooked up since freshman year," says Penny, grabbing her car keys and opening the front door.

"Cool," I say again, not sure why Penny thinks I care about that information.

"Yup," says Russ, holding open the door for me as the hot air hits my face and makes me want to run back inside. "We're right there in case you need anything."

"Great," I say, folding my arms across my chest.

I follow Penny and Chrissy out to the car. This is going to be a long night.

The place where we go, Shady Grove, is pretty great. We have to wait a few minutes for an outdoor table under this big tree (a pecan tree, Russ tells me), and there are hanging lights and wagon wheels and potted plants and the buzz of laughter all around. When we sit down, I see there's a huge menu, but I zero in on the tortilla fried catfish.

"There's a girl who knows how to order," says Russ when I tell the waiter what I want.

I give Russ an unamused smile, hoping to discourage further conversation.

I get off the hook for a while as Chrissy starts rambling about the trip she's going to take to Hawaii in the winter, and how she hopes the girls who rush Tri-Pi next year aren't "just in it for the glory." She and Penny have a serious back-and-forth about that while I try not to look incredulous. This is so not my scene.

After a few minutes, Russ brings the spotlight back to me.

"So, Priscilla, what's a Carolina girl doing this far west in the summertime?" he asks.

I have the urge to stab my fork into his big dumb hand. But it's not worth it to get into a "My name is Quinn!" fight with him—I probably won't see him again after tonight. At least, not if I can help it.

"I'm interning at Amalgam Records," I say, pleased with myself for having such a badass answer.

"Sweet, really?!" he says, his eyes lighting up. "Man, I've wanted to hang out at that place ever since I moved to Austin. How did you land that?"

"It was, uh, this really complicated process," I say, reaching for my iced tea and taking a big swig in the hopes that Chatty Chrissy will start talking about something else and distract everyone.

Gulp, gulp. They're all still looking at me expectantly.

"Yeah, you know," I continue. "It has to do with grades and my experience in the music scene in North Carolina and all that."

"That's super fun!" says Chrissy, leaning in on her elbows so the Tri-Pi lettering on her T-shirt is practically bouncing off the table.

"Are they paying you?"

"No," I say. "It's kind of like a volunteer thing. But, you know, highly selective volunteering."

"That's cool," says Russ. "When do you start?"

"Monday?" I say unconvincingly. I *think* I'm starting on Monday. It's not like I've had any confirmation since that middle-of-the-night phone commitment. But it seemed like a solid internship offer, right?

"You don't sound very sure," says Russ, leaning back as the waiter puts his meat loaf plate in front of him. Who orders meat loaf anyway? That's like what you beg your mom *not* to make for dinner. Yuck.

I give Russ an exasperated look. "I'm sure," I say. "Monday." I'm starting to sweat and I realize that it's very possible I'll come home with pit stains on my favorite Walters concert tee, which puts me in an even worse mood.

"You don't like to smile very much, do you, Priscilla?" Russ asks rhetorically, shaking his head and chuckling as he looks down at his messy plate.

"Not at some people," I say testily, digging into my fish.

"You look about as mean as that catfish probably used to," says Russ, still grinning.

He catches my eye for a moment and I suppress a chuckle—I have to give him props for a pretty good insult, but I'm not going to laugh out loud at my own expense.

By the end of dinner, Russ has slung precisely three more barbs my way, two of them witty enough to make me crack a smile. If I didn't know any better, I'd think he was flirting with me. He is undeniably hot in that generic kind of way—great body, huge smile, flashing dimples, and those deep blue eyes—but he's such a frat boy. I could never fall for someone like that. And besides, he's infuriating to talk to.

Just as we're leaving, a band starts setting up outside.

"It's Southern Cuz," says Chrissy excitedly, pausing by the exit.

"Just like Priscilla and Penny . . . cousins from Dixie." Russ grins. "We should stay."

We stand there for another minute while the band plugs in and tunes up, but when the first strains of the opening song start, I know I have to leave.

I tug on Penny's arm. "I hate country music," I whisper through clenched teeth.

"What?" she asks, clapping her hands to the beat and hardly turning around.

"I hate country music!" I shout, way too loudly. The back half of the restaurant turns to scowl at me.

I look over at Russ and he's nodding at me knowingly, like that bit of information doesn't surprise him.

"What?" I ask. "I just don't like it."

"Maybe you don't know enough about it," he says, challenging me. "Come on, ladies, let's get Priscilla here home so she can tune out the world with her iPod and listen to the Walters. Again."

On the drive back to the condo complex, I am fuming. Russ just totally dismissed my opinion and practically called me a musical ignoramus. I bet I know way more than he does.

When we get home, I jump out of the car and sprint up to Penny's door, holding my copy of the house key. My cousin waves good night to Chrissy and Russ.

"Great to meet you, Quinn!" shouts Chrissy, and I give her a quick wave in return.

"Night, Priscilla," says Russ.

Hmph.

"I'm glad you guys all get along," says Penny when we get inside.

Is she blind?

"Chrissy pretty much lives here half the time," she continues. "And Russ loves my place because I have a bigger TV than they do and nicer furniture."

Not in the dog's room, I think.

"Yeah," I say, not wanting to cause trouble. "They seem okay."

It doesn't matter what I think about her friends because I don't plan to spend much time hanging around here. As soon as I start my internship and meet more of my kind of people, I have a feeling I'll hardly ever be at Penny's. Then I won't have to deal with that exasperating Russ.

When I snuggle down onto my couch bed

that night, headphones in place, I dream of the angst-filled and sensitive lead singer (or guitarist . . . or drummer . . . or keyboardist . . . or, ooh, maybe a lead-singing keyboardist) who awaits me once I get to work at Amalgam Records.

Chapter 4

Penny lets me borrow her car for my first day at Amalgam, although I'm going to have to figure out an alternate form of transportation at some point. I guess I assumed the bus system in Austin would be amazing or at least serviceable, but I was wrong. Yesterday I spent all afternoon trying to get across town, and I got lost four times. I think I need a car.

Thank goodness, Penny isn't territorial about her BMW. It was nice to drive today, even though I'm embarrassed as I step out of the cherry red Beamer. How eighties-movie prep can I get?

Amalgam Records is in the middle of a row of stores that includes a Michael's crafts and a Kerr Drugs. That kind of surprises me. I mean, I wasn't picturing some LA–style round skyscraper, but a strip mall?

As I push open the glass door with AMAL-GAM spelled out in worn orange lettering, I realize my heart is speeding up a little bit. Maybe I should have called again to confirm the internship. What if they turn me away? I'm wearing a thrift-store T-shirt that says SIP AND SAIL TAVERN, ONEONTA, NY. I've never been to Oneonta, New York, let alone the bar, but the mustard yellow color of the shirt—combined with its just-worn-enough softness—makes it a favorite. I hope I look right. But not in a way that makes it seem like I *tried* to look right.

"Hey," I say to the girl who's sitting on the blue industrial carpet near the entrance. She's got huge, open brown eyes and thin lips, and her head looks somehow too big for her body. Her long dyed-red hair is shaggy and unkempt, but in a cool way, like she just stayed up all night and rolled into work. Actually, that's what her eye makeup looks like too—smudged around the edges but still luminous.

"Hey," she says back, not smiling. She's sitting among a bunch of cardboard boxes full of CDs, and she has a few cases spread out in front of her. "Who're you?"

"I'm Quinn Parker," I say, hoping my name means something to her. "I'm the summer intern."

She looks at me warily. "*I'm* the summer intern," she says.

Just then, a scruffy guy in corduroys and a white cotton undershirt comes through the front door.

"Are the demos in order, Jade?" he asks, not looking at me.

"Almost," she says.

"Good. Because I need to have them ready for—" Then he stops and glances over at me. "Who're you?" he asks.

It's the question of the morning. I try to stand tall, like I belong here, but that's getting more uncertain by the minute.

"I'm Quinn Parker," I say. "Um, is Rick around?" I invoke the only name that I have, the only evidence of my late-night-phone-call arrangement.

"I'm Rick," says Shaggy Man, who is definitely

too old to be my indie Supreme. He must be at least thirty.

"Oh," I start. "Well, I called a couple of weeks ago and set up this internship for the summer with someone, and he said I could start today and to ask for Rick so I'm just—"

Ramble much?

"Wait, wait—" Rick laughs and mercifully interrupts me. "Did you call really late at night?"

"Yes!" I say, dorkily hopeful. "That was me!"

"Oh, man," he says, sitting down atop one of the many cardboard boxes near Jade. "I thought that was my sister's friend joking around." He slaps his hand on his leg like something is so funny.

"We really only need one intern," Rick continues. "We're not a big operation here."

I look down at the blue carpet, not sure what to say. I should have called again. Who just shows up at an internship without any details? I was so excited to be offered the job, I guess I wanted to believe it would work out. If this internship falls through I don't know what I'll do. I want to tell him that I'm a huge fan of all the bands on Amalgam. I start spontaneously imagining all the things I would do for this job: 1) I would go on coffee runs. 2) I would organize closets. 3) I would carry band gear — anything it takes. But I'm afraid that eagerly voicing my obsessive list might not be cool. So all I do is look at him. I can feel that my eyes are a little desperate.

Jade is giving me an intense stare. I can feel that too.

Rick looks around at the pile of packages around him.

"Well, Mondays are pretty hectic," he says, scratching his chin stubble. "Jade here can probably use a hand unpacking and organizing. And there's a big festival we're working on for the beginning of August, so around then we might need more hands. Right, Jade?"

I look down at Jade and smile.

She shrugs. "Whatever," she says.

"Sweet," says Rick, standing up to shake my hand. "Welcome to Amalgam, Quinn the late-night caller."

"Thanks!" I say, allowing myself a huge beaming smile.

"Just Mondays, now," he says. "There's only one intern desk, and Jade here's been working on it for a while."

"No problem, sir," I say. Oooh, *sir*? That word sounds so stupid out loud.

He laughs and shakes his head as he walks by us to the back part of the office.

I notice Jade's also shaking her head. But not laughing. She looks up at me with those gorgeously messy eyes.

"Well, sit down and start unpacking!" she snaps.

I join her on the floor and grab a pair of scissors to open up my first box. I don't care if she's mad. I am officially official. Well, on Mondays. *Yes!*

Jade warms up to me slowly as I help her get everything in order. She tells me that she grew up in west Texas, and that her older brother's band used to be on Amalgam, before they split up. She'd always wanted to check out Austin, so her brother helped her set up this internship and she's staying in his apartment while he's on a solo tour for the summer. "I've already been here for a month," she says.

She explains to me that on Mondays, there are usually a bunch of packages—demos from wannabe Amalgam bands, inventory shipments that need to be cataloged for the music closet, and general inquiries from fans and managers.

"It's like the big mail day," she says. "And I guess Rick's right—I *can* use the help. On Mondays."

It's very clear to me that I'm going to have to find something else to occupy my time Tuesday through Friday this summer.

We alphabetize Amalgam CDs, file fan letters in "To Read" folders on top of the desk, and make a stack of new artist demos.

When we get to an advance copy of the Walters' new album, I jump up.

"The Walters are my favorite band," I say.

"Uh, that's cool," says Jade, grabbing the CD from my hand. "This is top secret though, so . . ."

"Oh, sure," I say. "I mean, I wasn't going to take it or anything."

Jade silently goes back to opening boxes.

"But do you think we could maybe listen to it?" I ask. I can't help myself.

"Calm down, fan-girl," says Jade. "Maybe later we can ask Rick, okay?"

"Okay," I say. "I love opening all this stuff, by the way." I really mean it. There are new bands to discover in every package, amazingly decorated fan letters, and mailings about every show in town.

"It gets old," she says.

"You're jaded," I say.

"No, I'm Jade," she replies, making a serious face.

We both burst out laughing then, and the slight tension that's remained between us seems cleared.

"I'm from North Carolina," I say, realizing that Jade hasn't asked me a single question since we've been sitting here, but I'm ready to talk to her more now that the ice is broken.

"Cool," she says, not paying much attention.

"Yeah, so I'm down here staying with my cousin Penny in her condo," I say. "But I have to sleep on the couch because her cross-dressing dog has the second bedroom."

"What?" asks Jade, suddenly interested.

"Seriously!" I say. "Penny's this huge sorority girl at UT with metallic Tri-Pi letters and a rush book and the requisite little white dog even!"

Jade laughs. "Penny sounds like a total character," she says.

"I don't know how I'm going to make it this summer," I say, feeling slightly guilty about dissing Penny with the first stranger I meet, but also relieved to have someone to talk to who might understand my objections.

"You can hang out with me if you want," says Jade nonchalantly. "I mean, I'm not from Austin, but I know the scene here. Amalgam people have to go to a lot of shows and stuff."

"Yeah, cool," I say. Inside, I'm ecstatic. I think I just made my first real friend here.

"So do you have a boyfriend?" asks Jade as we walk outside to a taco stand at the edge of the parking lot to grab some lunch.

"Nope," I say, choosing a fish taco and a Coke while Jade gets a bean burrito.

We sit down on the parking lot curb to eat,

and I decide to trust Jade a little more.

"I actually really want to meet a guy here," I say.

"Ooh, yeah," says Jade. "Summer fling."

I laugh. "I guess," I say. "I just never really found my type of guy back in North Carolina, and I thought maybe Austin would be the perfect place, since there's such a great music scene and lots of smart band guys."

"There are also lots of frat boys," says Jade. She takes a big bite of her burrito.

"I've already met one of those," I say, thinking of Russ and his irksome personality.

"They're not all bad," she says. "Just mostly."

I put my taco down as sauce drips on my arm. I grab a napkin and wipe it up, then I gaze across the parking lot.

"I can picture him," I say, probably sounding too wistful for my own good.

"Your dream guy?" Jade asks, smirking.

"Yeah," I say. "I guess that sounds dumb." I pick up my taco.

"No, it doesn't," she says. "Do tell."

"Okay," I say, carefully finishing my chew

before I lapse into the vision I have. "Dark hair and perfectly hip glasses—meaning either black frame classics or those larger, slightly tinted ones that Alpha girls think are nerdy but that I know are truly stylish."

Jade laughs encouragingly. "Go on," she says.

"He loves the Walters, of course, but he also knows a lot of other bands that he can introduce me to," I say. "I really want to hear new stuff and fall in love with the music he worships. We can go to shows every night and make each other playlists, and choose one song that's just ours, just for this summer, that we'll both always remember."

"You are such a spaz!" says Jade, standing up and tossing out her burrito wrapper.

I stand up too. "Oh, and he's in a band," I say, walking across the parking lot and back to Amalgam. "Or he's a DJ. I could completely fall for an indie-rock DJ."

Jade's face lights up.

"What?" I ask as she holds open the door to the office for me.

"I've got someone you need to meet," she

says mysteriously. "Don't make plans for Friday night."

I try to press her for the rest of the day, but she won't tell me who this "need to meet" person is . . . although she does tell me he's a guy. At the end of the day, she finally caves a little.

"His name is Sebastian," she says. "And he is smoking hot."

That's all I need to hear. I cannot wait for Friday.

Chapter 5

The rest of the week goes by really slowly. I realize that my assumption about Penny's grocery shopping habits was only partially correct. She does indeed shop, but she buys only fruit and candy. It's like this weird mix—apples, Sour Patch Kids, honeybell oranges, Sno-Caps, grapes, gummy bears, bananas . . . I may turn into a sugar-craving citrus animal if I don't get some protein soon.

I email Mom and Dad to tell them all about Amalgam and how much I'm going to learn about the "real world" this summer, leaving out the part about my internship being one day a week and my diet consisting of things that I'd eat if I were the love child of Willy Wonka and Chiquita Banana. I read a few guidebooks to Austin but realize that I have no way to get anywhere I want to go without a car. Penny has to use the BMW for the rest of the week, and I'd feel sheepish borrowing it all the time anyway.

Luckily, the condo's just a few blocks from campus, and by Friday afternoon, I've figured out the easiest way to walk there. I'm ready to leave my air-conditioned sanctuary. I think. I load up my backpack with my iPod, a snack (a honeybell), a blanket, and two books on my personal summer-reading list. Oh, and a big-ass bottle of water.

When I reach campus, my water's almost gone. I find a drinking fountain and refill my SIGG before I spread out on the first big stretch of grass I find. Under a tree. I can't risk getting sun, and I've never been into tanning. Besides, did I mention it's a thousand degrees outside? It is. There are lots of students around, but I'm sure the crowds are much bigger during the year. Summer is always the best season in a college town, when the student population thins out a little.

"Hey, hey, Priscilla!" I hear a deep twang behind me. I guess the population hasn't thinned out enough.

"Russ," I say, pulling out my headphones and tucking my iPod into my bag so he won't see that I'm listening to the Walters.

He sits down on the edge of my blanket by my outstretched feet. As if he's welcome. I remember that Penny told me that Russ is on campus most days, finishing up some paper for a class, which he didn't turn in on time last semester—he needs it to become a senior next year.

"Haven't seen you around this week," he says. "You been working hard at Amalgam?"

"Yeah," I say. "It keeps me busy."

"So, are you riding the bus all the way to South Congress every day?" he asks, naming the street Amalgam is on.

I wonder how much I should lie here. I look back at him.

His smile widens and he swats my out-stretched foot, knocking off my flip-flop. Then he laughs and lies down on his back in the grass at my feet, raising his arms to cross his hands behind his head. *How often does he have to work out to get that kind of bicep definition?*

"I know you're only there on Mondays,"

says Russ. "Penny told me."

"Well, I worked really hard on Monday," I say defensively, chastising myself internally for even noticing his sculpted muscles. "And I've been busy the rest of the week."

"So busy you can't even come next door to hang out?" he asks, leaning up on one arm and looking at me sideways. He tucks a blade of grass in his mouth and starts to chew on it. Like a cow.

"I've had my own stuff going on," I say. The truth is, "my own stuff" has been a lot of time online with my headphones on. When Penny goes out, she always invites me, but Chrissy and the Tri-Pis are not my people. Nor is Russ for that matter. I've been bonding with Miss Tiara though—she nuzzles next to me on the couch while I listen to music. And I have to agree with Penny: She does seem happiest in dresses.

"Fair enough, Priscilla," says Russ, lying back again with a maddening grin. "But I don't think you want to spend all summer stuck in that apartment."

"What are you suggesting?" I ask. Because, well, I sort of agree with him.

"You must have some money saved up if you're working a no-pay internship," he says. "Why don't I take you down to Albie's to get yourself a beater."

"A what?" I ask.

"A beater," he says, still staring at the sky and chewing on that mutilated blade of grass. "A clunker of a car you can drive around for the summer and sell back to him in August when you leave."

I consider the idea. It's not a bad one, and I do feel stuck at Penny's condo. I have about two thousand dollars saved up for the summer from my movie theater job in North Carolina. I cannot explain what it takes to save two thousand dollars on minimum wage, but let's just call it two years of popcorn shifts and very little new clothing.

"I could probably spend like five hundred dollars," I say, calculating things in my head.

"That'll get you something nice at Albie's," he says, sitting up to face me. Then he starts explaining that Albie is this old guy who lives outside of town and has a lot full of eclectic cars.

In the mottled sunlight through the trees, Russ looks like an old movie star, someone out of a Western who belongs on a horse with a gun slung around his waist. But here he is, on my blanket in the shade. And when he's not being obnoxious, he's kind of . . .

"You hungry?" he asks, interrupting my inappropriate daydream and finally spitting out that blade of grass.

"Starving," I say, feeling friendly toward Russ for the first time. *He's not a bad guy, he's just not my type,* I remind myself.

"I thought maybe the grape-and-grape-NERDS diet Penny lives on might not work for a girl like you who enjoys her tortilla-fried catfish," he says, standing up and offering me his hand.

I laugh. He remembered what I ordered last week.

"Let's go get some real food," he says.

After a huge burger that tastes like heaven, Russ asks me if I want to hang out tonight. The weird thing is, I don't fully want to say no. But I have to.

"I've got plans," I say. Tonight is the night I meet Sebastian the DJ. I've already made him my summer fling . . . in my own mind anyway. I even IMed with Raina about it last night, and she agreed that with a name like Sebastian, he has to be The Supreme.

"That's cool," says Russ, yawning and stretching his arms over his head as we finish our walk back to the condo. "So I'll come over tomorrow morning and we'll go to Albie's to car-shop. Remember to get out some cash tonight — he doesn't take credit cards."

"Okay," I say.

"It's a date," he says, walking up to his door while I head to mine.

"Well, it's not a *date*," I clarify.

"Relax, Priscilla," he says, smiling and shaking his head. "It's just an expression."

I sigh audibly in frustration. *Why can't he just call me Quinn?!* I slam the door and I can hear his loud, whooping laugh through the wall.

I stomp up the stairs to take a long shower while Penny's not here. As much as I hate to admit it, I enjoy the amount of product she has in her bathroom. I get to choose between four pairings of shampoo and conditioner, not to mention three scents of body wash and six (*six!*) facial cleansers. If I approved of such excess, I'd really get into this. But I don't. Well, at least not in theory.

When I go downstairs to get dressed, I plug my iPod into the stereo. I almost put on the Walters, but I wonder if Russ can hear through the walls. I choose Seasick Pandas instead and turn up the volume. Their fast-paced guitar riffs put me in a dancing mood as I pull on my favorite pair of faded jeans and a free shirt that I got when I subscribed to *NYLON* magazine last year. It's white with hot pink lettering, and I cut out the neckline a little bit and washed it a ton of times to make it stretchy and a little faded. I love free shirts.

I sneak back upstairs to put some of Penny's various volume-gel-hair-thickening-beach-texture gunk in my hair, which has faded to a pale greenish-blue hue and is growing out a little. When I try out some light mascara and a slash of dark red lipstick, I notice that Miss Tiara is in the bathroom with me, her head cocked sideways.

"What?" I ask her. "I may not be Party Penny's style of hot, but I think I look good."

Miss Tiara barks her approval. Or disapproval. Who can tell? Either way, I feel ready for tonight. I go downstairs and sit on my couchbed, awaiting Jade.

The hanging-around-to-be-picked-up time after getting ready to go out is always a buzzkill. I grab some candy from my cousin's overflowing jar in the kitchen and suck on a Sugar Daddy to keep my energy up.

Finally, the doorbell rings. I leave a quick note for Penny telling her not to wait up, and I head into the night for my first Austin music experience.

Chapter 6

At Dirty's, the scene is all pool tables and neon beer signs, despite the fact that Friday night is eighteen and older, so everyone can enjoy the DJs. There's a dartboard in the corner and a row of arcade games along one wall.

When we get there, I immediately notice him despite all the lit-up distractions. Sebastian. It's like a spotlight is shining on the DJ booth.

"I see him!" I say to Jade excitedly.

"That's probably because there's a spotlight on the DJ booth," she says.

Riiight. I silently acknowledge that I could possibly be a little overexcited here.

"Introduce me!" I say.

"Oh, I don't *know* him," she says. "I just thought he matched your description perfectly."

And he does. Black hair smoothed out into

a hipster cut that hangs in a wavy line around his face, almost covering his intense green eyes, which are framed by large oval glasses with a dark olive-colored edge. He looks like an album cover for a band I'd really like.

Jade's tugging my arm over to the DJ booth. But without her intro, how will I ever get up the nerve to—

"I'm Jade. And this is Quinn." I guess Jade has nerve enough for both of us.

"Sebastian," nods the DJ, barely looking up from his vinyl. He hasn't started spinning yet— he's laying out his selections for the night.

I glance at the albums he has out—Remote Storage, Paper Prospect, Cakewalk, plus an old David Bowie single and some Cure songs mixed in. I think I'm in love.

"What's this band?" I ask, pointing to an Endless Rain album and looking up at his effortlessly cool face. At this point, the only thing I'm confident enough to ask him about is music.

"Dance tunes," he says. "But dark."

"Like Depeche Mode?" I ask, liking how he keeps his sentences short.

He looks at me then and grins, showing

crooked teeth that give him that just-off-enough-to-look-perfect smile. "Kind of," he says.

"Come talk to us when you get a break," says Jade, tugging me away.

"What are you doing?!" I ask when we get to a table and sit down. "Did you see him smiling at me?"

"You have to leave him wanting more," says Jade instructively. "Besides, he's working and you're not here to see him, you're here to enjoy the music. Studied nonchalance is the key to catching an indie boy."

She's good at this, I realize.

While Jade and I talk about random things, I surreptitiously watch Sebastian's shiny black hair move back and forth as he changes tracks from his booth. I appreciate the way his long, thin fingers carefully tuck each record into its cover after it spins, and I think how gentle those hands must be. I get a little shiver each time he does it.

After an hour, the live band is getting ready to start, so Sebastian packs up his stuff.

Please come over to us, please come over to us. I keep my face calm as I see his long stride, out of the corner of my eye, heading for our table.

"Hey," he says, sitting down in a conveniently empty third chair that we had discouraged others from stealing during his set with "don't touch it" glares.

"Hey," I say.

"I'm thirsty," says Jade-the-expert-wingwoman, getting up to go to the bar. "Be right back."

"You new in town?" asks Sebastian, turning his full attention on me.

"Yeah," I say. "I'm from North Carolina, but I'm here for the summer."

I want to tell him I'm working at Amalgam, but I also don't want to be name-dropping right away.

"Doesn't your friend work for Amalgam?" he asks. Guess that takes care of that.

"Yeah," I say. "We met there—I'm an intern."

"Cool," he says. "My favorite bands are on that label."

"Mine too," I say. "The Walters."

"They are wild," says Sebastian. "Those guys put on a show."

"I know," I say. "I've seen them seventeen times."

"Whoa!" He laughs. "You're a superfan."

"Kind of," I say, embarrassed.

"It's cool," he says. "I am too. That's why I spin—I just love getting into all those songs and figuring out the mix that will set the perfect mood for the band that's playing after my set. Like tonight Inconceivable Hat is here, so I wanted to spin some old influences that I hear when they perform."

"That's really smart," I say, leaning on my elbow and watching Sebastian's mouth move. He's talking with his hands now that he's explaining what he spins, and they look even softer up close.

Jade comes back with her drink and breaks my reverie, but she's careful to be low-key and let me and Sebastian do most of the back-and-forth.

Talking with him turns out to be easy. We like a lot of the same bands, and he is complete physical perfection. Even his flaws, like the way one of his front bottom teeth overlaps the other and how one strand of hair is slightly longer than the rest on the left side of his head, make him somehow more attractive.

When we leave around midnight, Sebastian writes his cell number in a matchbook, which strikes me as romantic and iconic and so much cooler and less presumptuous than actually programming it into my phone. I clench it in my hand as I get into Jade's old Toyota and watch him speed away on a green Vespa.

"How cool is he?" I ask rhetorically.

"Told you so," says Jade.

I fall asleep that night dreaming of those vinyl-changing hands.

Chapter 7

I wake up to the smell of coffee and the sound of Penny's humming. I go upstairs to shower away the mascara remains from last night. I usually kind of like that raccoon-eye look, but today I feel like being clean.

I put on an old T-shirt that says ALLEN AND SONS BARBECUE and my jean shorts, which Penny was totally right about — I'm wearing them almost exclusively now because of the heat. Then I go downstairs and join my cousin in the kitchen, where she's picking at a mixed berry bowl.

"What's up, Quinn?" she asks, feeding a strawberry to Miss Tiara, who sits on a barstool between us at the kitchen island.

"Nothing," I say, tucking my hair behind my ears.

"What'd you do last night?" she asks.

"I just went out with a friend from work," I say. "We saw a show."

"Fun!" says Penny.

"Yeah, it was cool," I say. I don't want to tell her about Sebastian, because I can't picture them getting along. If I admit it to myself, I think I'd be embarrassed to let him meet her, in all her sorority-sister glory.

"Sorry I've been MIA all week," says Penny. "Planning Rush is a huge task, and I'm also trying to get a head start on a venue for Tri-Pi's first formal of the year, the Sweet September Swingfest."

"It's okay," I say, cringing internally at the name of the dance. "I can entertain myself."

"I know," says Penny. "But I just feel bad that you don't have a car and—"

Ding-dong. Penny jumps up to get the door as Miss Tiara starts barking haughtily.

I race to head them off. "I'll get it," I say.

Russ is standing outside in the sun with a huge grin on his face. His curls are completely unruly today, I notice. "Ready?" he asks.

"Ready," I say. "See you later, Penny."

Her mouth drops open, and so does Miss Tiara's.

"Russ is taking me to buy a car," I explain. "I was just about to tell you. Bye!"

I shut the door before Penny can say anything. It's not a big deal. I really hate it when people act all like, *Ooooh*, about things. We're not in first grade.

Outside, Russ opens up the passenger side door to a giant Ford truck that looks like it's seen a few decades. "This one's yours?" I ask.

"You surprised?" asks Russ, taking my hand to help me step up into the cab. I swat him away. I can do this myself.

"I'm actually not surprised," I say. I should have known that this old rusty truck, among all the other normal cars in the lot, would belong to Russ.

We drive through the main part of town by the Capitol building and then head out onto an empty stretch of road. I'm guessing they didn't have AC in cars made in the 1950s or whenever this thing came from, so we have the windows rolled down, and the engine isn't the quietest in the world. Despite all the noise and wind, the fields around us look peaceful and still, and I lean back in the seat and stare over the horizon. It might be one of the only times in my life when there isn't music playing, but I feel perfectly content.

After a few minutes, Russ slows down in front of a giant old barn surrounded by broken-down-looking cars. I'm sad the drive is over, to be honest, and also that the wind is no longer keeping me cool. The heat feels like a hot blanket clinging tightly to my body.

I step down onto a dusty driveway, and Russ puts two fingers in his mouth to whistle. It is *loud*.

"That's a skill I never learned," I say to him.

"It's handy," he says, smiling down at me. "Here comes Albie."

"Y'all want a piña colada?" shouts the old man walking up to us. He's wearing faded blue overalls and a T-shirt that may at one point have been white but is now covered in dust and rust. I'm into his look.

"Nah," says Russ, though a frosty drink sounds kind of good to me. "We're trying to find Quinn here a car."

I look at Russ sideways. *Did he just call me Quinn?* He winks.

"Hello, Quinn," says Albie, holding out his hand.

"Hey there," I say, reaching out to shake.

"Come sit," he says.

Russ and I follow him to a circle of tree stumps behind the barn, where we each take a seat. I look at Russ like, *What's going on?* But he just smiles and nods, like this is all part of the process with Albie.

"So, Quinn, tell me about yourself," says Albie.

I'm not sure what to say, so I start with something easy.

"I'm really into music," I say. "I came down here from North Carolina to intern at Amalgam Records and I love it so far."

Albie nods. "And how did you and Russ hook up?" he asks.

"We didn't hook up!" I say.

Russ laughs at my reaction. "He means how'd we meet," he says.

I feel stupid for a minute, I guess I'm being

a little jumpy. Older people don't say "hook up" that way. But I recover quickly. "My cousin Penny lives next door to Russ," I say. "They're friends and we met through her."

"And you came down here without a car?" asks Albie.

"I thought the bus would be better," I admit. "And Penny has a car, so—"

"That the one with the shiny BMW?" Albie asks, looking at Russ.

"Yup," says Russ, and they both chuckle.

"That your kind of ride?" Albie asks me. "A shiny BMW?"

"No, sir," I say. "I'd just like something that gets good gas mileage and is reliable. I was actually considering a Vespa because I saw someone on one last night and thought that might be a good option."

Russ and Albie look at each other and start to howl with laughter. "A Vespa?!" says Russ.

"I don't even quite know what that is," says Albie, wiping tears from his eyes.

There sure seems to be a lot of cackling at my expense going on. I'm not convinced Albie's such a good car salesman.

"Vespas are for tools," says Russ. "Seriously, Priscilla."

Ooh, he makes me so mad with his "Priscilla" crap! "Well, just because you have a vintage truck doesn't mean we all have to be driving around using completely irresponsible amounts of gas and creating noise pollution everywhere!" I shout, trying to shut Russ up.

"I like my car," he says slowly and firmly.

I like it too, truth be told, but I'm not about to admit that in this moment.

"Let's not fight," says Albie, putting his hands on his knees and hoisting himself off the stump. "Let's look at some automobiles."

An hour and one test-drive down the dirt road later, I hand Albie four hundred dollars in cash for a 1993 Ford Festiva. It's yellow and rusty, and the clutch sticks a little, but it's exactly what I want. And it's the first car he showed me. "It looks like you," Albie says. I'm not sure how to take that, but I'm thinking it's a compliment.

"You gonna be able to work that clutch all

the way to town?" asks Russ, climbing into his truck.

"Watch me," I say, taking off in front of him. It feels good to be in the driver's seat.

When we get back to the condo, I am fully exhilarated. The Festiva drives really well, and I feel in total control with a stick shift. At home, I inherited my mom's old Honda, but this is a new experience: I just bought a car!

I park it next to Penny's BMW, and when I get out to admire it, I have to say that I think my little yellow beater looks much cooler than her sorority-mobile. I'm smiling when Russ pulls into the lot. I'm over being annoyed with him now that I have my new ride.

"You're a good driver," he says, tipping his baseball hat at me.

"Thanks," I say. "Are you surprised?"

"Not really," he says, walking up to stand next to me and take another look at the Festiva.

"So now I can go anywhere I want to," I say.

"And where is it that you want to go?" Russ asks.

"Nowhere particular," I say. "I just mean to shows and stuff. I have to see a lot of music for my job." At least, I hope I have to see a lot of music for my job.

"Oh, right," he says, laughing a little. "I guess that's what you did last night."

I don't say anything. I don't have to tell him what I'm doing—he's just the neighbor. I mean, it was nice of him to help me get a car, but he's Penny's friend, not mine.

Russ walks around the side of the car and peers inside.

"Classic!" He chuckles.

"What?" I ask, ready to defend whatever he's making fun of.

"This thing has a tape player," he says.

"Yeah," I say. "I noticed that. I was thinking I could buy one of those adapter thingies and plug in my iPod. They have those, right?"

"Don't do that," says Russ, looking disappointed. "Have some sense of nostalgia. Listen to a tape."

"I don't have any," I say, and it's true. I don't

know if I've ever owned a tape.

"Stay there," says Russ, sprinting into his apartment. He comes out a minute later and hands me a dusty Memorex with no cover.

"What's this?" I ask.

"You'll find out on your next car ride," he says.

Chapter 8

On Monday when I drive to work, I put in Russ's tape. It's this guy singing in kind of a high voice about a speeding motorcycle—not what I was expecting. It's bizarrely cool, but I'm not sure who or what it is.

Jade's at the desk when I get to work.

"Guess who called," she says as I walk in.

"The Walters?" I ask excitedly.

"Better," she says. "Sebastian."

"He called *you*?" I ask, feeling my stomach drop.

"No, twerp!" she says. "He called Amalgam. He wants to come by this week and drop off a demo of his friend's band. I told him you'd be here today only."

"You did not!" I say, my face getting hot. "Did you?"

"Of course," says Jade. "I could tell you're the reason he wants to come by."

"Oh, well, that's cool," I say, trying to put on my nonchalant face.

"You're so excited," Jade says, smiling slyly. "I love it."

I just grin at her and start opening boxes. When Rick comes in around noon, most of the mail is unpacked.

"Hey, guys," he says, scratching the back of his bedhead. "This looks pretty under control. Nice work."

"Thanks," says Jade. "Quinn is a big help."

She shoots me a smile.

"And we were wondering . . ." Jade continues, "if we could listen to the new Walters album that came in last week?"

"Oh, yeah!" says Rick. "Let's put it on."

I guess the album's not so secret after all. I mouth a "thank you" to Jade when Rick goes into the back. He brings out a CD and pops it into the stereo on Jade's desk. Then he grabs a rolling chair from his office and joins the two of us as Jade cranks up the volume.

When the music starts, I lean back against an unpacked box. The melodies rush over me and I close my eyes. What's really nice is that Rick and Jade both are doing the same thing, I see, when I peek once around track three. They're completely still, taking it in, really appreciating the music. They're even looking at each other, like they're sharing this intense moment through the Walters. Not chattering over it or doing something else while the songs are in the background—they love it like I do. I can feel it.

Suddenly, what I feel is a rush of heat as the front door opens. I open my eyes and see Sebastian there. His pale face looks soft in the afternoon light, and his smile gives me a chill despite the hundred-degree air blast he just let in through the door. Then, track six starts. I hope it's a good one.

"Hey there," says Sebastian, staring at me. He glances at Rick and Jade. We must look really zoned out. I stand up to say hi, but then I'm not sure if I should shake his hand or what, so I shift my weight awkwardly. Luckily, Rick stands up too.

"Hey, man," Rick says, slapping Sebastian on the back.

"Hey, Rick, I just brought by this demo by a friend of mine's band," says Sebastian. "They're called Inspired by Ross. I've been spinning this one track for a couple of weeks and people are really into it, but they're not signed yet."

Of course Sebastian knows Rick. *He's that cool*, I think.

"Sweet," says Rick, taking the CD. "Listen, I have to get some stuff done, but let's finish this Walters party later. Thanks for dropping this by, Sebastian." Rick walks into the back office.

Sebastian just stands there for a second, and it looks like he's about to leave. I'm trying to think of something to say to make him stay, but then he turns to me. "So, do you guys get a lunch break or something?" he asks.

"We do!" says Jade, standing up from her desk and talking rapidly. "I have to run some errands. I'm sure Quinn is hungry though. Right, Q?"

Best. Wingwoman. Ever.

"Sure," I say. "Let me get my bag."

I follow Sebastian outside and I take in the view. He's wearing a black Luminous Energy '07 tour T-shirt with the arms cut off and a pair of tight black jeans. His shoes are pointy leather boots. He looks like a rock star as he swings one leg over his Vespa. He puts on his blue helmet and grabs a smaller white one from the back of the bike.

"Hop on," he says.

The wind-in-my-hair feeling in Russ's truck was nothing compared to this hurricane of a ride. I have my hands around Sebastian's waist as we weave through traffic and round sharp turns with a gentle lean. I gasp audibly as we take a left into a parking lot. We end up at the same burger place where Russ and I ate last week.

"Are you a vegetarian?" asks Sebastian.

"Not even slightly," I say, handing him my helmet. I have the urge to shout out a "Whoop!" after that ride, but I know that wouldn't be cool. So instead, I just shake out my short hair to release some of the thrill I'm feeling.

"This place has a lot of vegetarian options,"

he says. "Just in case. I've been off meat for a few years."

"Cool," I say, thinking about the fantastic burger I had last week and how he's really missing out. But I don't mention that.

When we walk in, Sebastian chooses a corner booth and we order sodas. They come in huge glasses full of ice, and I'm planning on getting at least two free refills. "Have you ever been to Europe?" asks Sebastian.

I think I know where he's going with this, so I say, "Yeah, I went to England the summer I was eight because my dad had a conference in Oxford. And when you order a Coke they give you a tiny glass with no ice!"

Sebastian looks at me strangely. "Oh, yeah," he says. "I guess they do do that. But I was going to ask you what your favorite city in Europe is."

"I've only been to London and Oxford," I say, wondering if he'll think I'm uncultured or something because I haven't been to, like, Berlin or Paris.

"That's cool," he says, and then he reaches over to grab his napkin with that soft right hand that changes albums when he spins. I feel a flutter in my stomach.

"Hey, hey, Priscilla." I feel a knot in my stomach.

I look over my shoulder to see Russ sauntering toward our booth.

"Who's your friend?" he asks, and I see a weird look in his eye, but just for a second.

"This is Sebastian," I say. I so don't want to introduce them, but there's no way out. I'm trapped.

"Hey," says Sebastian, nodding at Russ.

"And how do you two know each other?" asks Russ, like he's my dad or something.

"We met at Dirty's," says Sebastian. "I spin there on Friday nights."

"Huh," says Russ, chuckling as he folds his arms across his chest. His dimples are out in full force today. I think they're extra noticeable when he's mocking me.

"*What* are you laughing at?" I ask, annoyed.

"Leave it to Priscilla to find a DJ in a live-music town," he says, more to himself than to me.

"Who's Priscilla?" asks Sebastian.

"No one," I say, glaring up at Russ and sending intense "please leave" vibes his way.

"Well, y'all enjoy your lunch," he says. "See you later, Priscilla."

He turns and walks out the door, and I watch to make sure he's gone.

"Who was that?" asks Sebastian.

"My cousin's dumb fratty cowboy neighbor," I say. "In other words, no one."

"Harsh," says Sebastian, but he laughs too. "He did seem pretty fratty."

I try to enjoy the rest of our lunch, but I can't get Russ's annoying presence out of my head. *Why is he acting like he owns me or something? And why can't he just call me Quinn?!*

Sebastian doesn't ask about the "Priscilla" thing again, and I'm glad. I tell him how Penny is a spoiled princess with a silly little dog, and he tells me about music and the places he's been. Then he says we should get together again this weekend.

When the check comes, Sebastian says he'll cover it, even though I offer to pay. He leaves a twenty on our nineteen-dollar total.

"Oh, cool, I'll leave the rest of the tip," I say.

"Nah," says Sebastian, waving my three ones away. "That guy wasn't a great waiter."

I grin, but after Sebastian turns his back to walk out, I put down three more dollars in cash. I'm not into the low-tipping thing.

Still, everything else about lunch was so nice. My summer plan to snag an indie boyfriend is going perfectly. Except for one fratty fly in the ointment. A fly I'm determined to ignore.

I drive around in my car during the week—it's the only time I wish I had long, flowing, Hollywood hair. With the windows down and the music cranked up, I feel like I'm in the middle of a song. Maybe even a country song, but not one of those whiny wife-left-me-dog-died songs—a good one.

I've been listening to the tape Russ passed off, since it's the only form of music I have for the car, and I have to admit that it's growing on me. I found out that the guy with the weird high voice is Daniel Johnston, a musician who's lived in Austin and inspired people like Kurt Cobain in the early nineties. Daniel's an artist too, and I even bought a T-shirt with a design he drew of a little alien frog who's saying, "Hi, How Are You?" It's kind of an Austin thing, the girl at the store told me.

The cost of gas — even in my little Festiva — is keeping me from going too far, though. By Friday, I'm so ready to get out of the condo and meet Sebastian at Dirty's. I wear my Daniel Johnston tee, and I meet Jade at the club.

"Nice shirt," she says.

I can't tell if she's being a little snide about it, but I decide it's a true compliment, because *I* am into it.

"Thanks," I say.

"How was your week?" she asks.

"About to get more interesting," I say, looking at the DJ booth where Sebastian is set up. He smiles and nods, then starts to spin. You know how when you're watching a guy perform, even if he's in a DJ booth instead of onstage, it's just incredibly sexy? People are focused on Sebastian like he's the ruler of Dirty's, and in some ways he is. He sets everyone's mood — upbeat and light, dark and moody, thoughtful and reflective. Song after song he makes great choices, and it's not an easy skill.

Eleven amazing tracks later, I'm in music heaven and Sebastian takes a break. He comes over to me and kisses my cheek before he slides into our semicircular booth. It's like he's *already* my boyfriend. I fight the urge to get giddy and girly.

"You guys are cute," says Jade, whipping out her phone and snapping a photo of us. "I'm emailing it to you for Facebook," she says to me.

Sebastian scoffs. "Don't tell me you're into social networking," he says, rolling his eyes.

"Just to keep in touch with my friends," I say, feeling self-conscious. The truth is, I live on Facebook. And it's been helping me deal with the bad TV that Penny watches almost every night.

"Those sites are for social retards," he says, which annoys me for a couple of reasons: 1) Because that's so not true, and all my friends are on Facebook. 2) Because "retards" just isn't a cool word to use.

But then he gives me a smile, like he's joking around with me, and my annoyance melts away.

When Sebastian goes back to his records, I peek at the photo. It's perfect—*he's* perfect. Floppy brown hair hanging over his glasses, pale, lanky arm around my shouder, ironic smile. He's exactly who I pictured for my summer fling. Now if I can just get the fling part going . . .

"Have you guys kissed yet?" asks Jade, reading my mind as I stare at the photo.

"Nope," I say. "But I'm going to fix that tonight."

"It shouldn't be too hard," she says, glancing in Sebastian's direction. "He looks pretty smitten."

I lock eyes with him and he gives me a small wave.

"So who's your summer prospect?" I look back at Jade, realizing that though we've talked extensively about my dream guy, she hasn't yet shared anything about hers.

"Who, me?" she asks.

"No, I'm talking to the imaginary girl on your left," I say.

"I'm a free bird, Quinn," she says. "I do not want to be locked down."

"Is a summer fling equivalent to a jail sentence?" I ask.

"For me it is!" she says, laughing. "I like being single."

"Whatever works," I say, but I wonder what her deal is. She changes the subject to whether she should go light or dark for her next nail polish change, and I let her drop the guy talk, for now.

A few minutes later, when Sebastian's set is over around midnight, Jade seems ready to leave. "I have to go," she says. "But you've got your car now, right? So . . ."

"It's fine," I say, worrying that my asking her about guys made her have a Cinderella complex. "I guess I'll see you later."

"Monday!" she says, calling out to me as she edges her way to the door. And then she's gone.

It's weird—Jade hasn't ever called me to hang out during the week, aside from the occasional midday burrito break. I know she's busy at Amalgam, but I'd definitely welcome a dinner out with her instead of fruit-and-candy plates at home with Penny and Chrissy while we watch reruns of *The Bachelor* on TV, which has become my nightly routine. I shrug. Maybe I'll try to get her to open up a little more at work. Right now, I've got something else on my mind.

I walk over to Sebastian and help him stack his albums into a plastic carrying crate.

"How do you fit these on your Vespa?" I ask.

He laughs. "I don't," he says. "The owner lets me lock them up in the office here since it's my steady gig."

"That's convenient," I say, completely distracted. *Must get him to kiss me.* I send a *please-smooch-me* vibe in his direction.

We walk to the office and I follow him in through the locked door. He kicks it shut behind me, and as soon as he puts down the heavy crate, he spins around and grabs my waist. I almost drop my crate on the floor, but he shifts it from my hands to the desk and before I know it, we're kissing. And I don't mean the kind of kissing that is light and sporadic—I mean the kind that is full-on, deeply passionate, melt-me-in-your-arms making out. My vibe worked!

His hands are now on my hips and he pushes

me back against the metal desk in the corner. I sit on top of it, wrapping my legs easily around his waist. I've made out with guys before— I even had a six-month-long relationship in eleventh grade, and that guy convinced me to sleep with him before I realized he was bad news— but Sebastian is by far the hottest guy I've ever kissed. The band outside, My Almost Life, is playing a song called "Sweet and Lowdown" and I know I'll have to buy their CD so I can remember this moment.

After twenty minutes stuck together, a knock on the door makes us both freeze in place. Sebastian moves quickly to the other side of the room as I hop off the desk and straighten my shirt.

A guy named Mel walks in. At least, I think his name is Mel. He's wearing one of those bowling-league shirts with a name tag sewn onto it—but maybe he's just being ironic.

"Hey, Seb," he says to Sebastian. "Sorry to interrupt." He flashes one of those annoying *Heh-heh* smiles that macho guys give to each other, and Sebastian looks down.

There's a long pause and I realize Sebastian

isn't going to rescue us from this situation.

"That's okay," I say, slightly irked that I'm the one who has to ease the awkwardness. "We were just locking up some albums."

Then I grab Sebastian's arm and rush out of Mel's office. We walk past the bar and burst through the doors and out into the parking lot. One of the things I am not loving about Texas is how bursting through doors leads to instant heat as opposed to refreshing coolness. It's like that in North Carolina too, but not as intense. I start to sweat.

"Thanks," he says. "I got a little overcome in there."

"It's okay," I say, shaking off my irritation at having to save us from the awkwardness and taking his soft hand up to my face. "I liked it."

"So, I can call you this weekend?" asks Sebastian.

"You'd better," I say, moving in for one last taste of his lips. I'm in a bold mood. Even though I spent the last month of school plotting my Austin summer and exactly how I would get the perfect, music-filled, indie boyfriend . . . I didn't really think it would *work*. I watch Sebastian get on his Vespa and drive off. He gives me a one-handed wave and I do a little dance on the sidewalk—a happy shimmy. Then I go back inside to buy My Almost Life's CD—I *need* that song.

When I get home, I immediately change my profile song on MySpace to "Sweet and Lowdown," post the photo of me and Sebastian on Facebook, and then leave a note on Raina's wall telling her to check it out.

The next morning, I log in to Facebook again. The note Raina left says one word: "Supreme."

Chapter 9

By Tuesday night, not only has the elation that caused me to do the happy shimmy disappeared, but my usually stable confidence is also wavering. Sebastian has not called. It's been four days since our makeout session, not that I'm counting. In an attempt to *not* be like the ladies on *The Bachelor*, with whom I am intimately familiar after living with Penny, I haven't really expressed my disappointment to anyone. Well, unless you count Monday, when I responded to Jade's question about Sebastian by saying, "Guys are losers." She smiled sympathetically and said, "He'll call."

But he hasn't. And here I sit on Tuesday night in my pajamas with Penny, waiting to see if Brad from Season 11 is going to propose.

"This one is a *shocker*!" says Penny, hugging

Miss Tiara tightly in her arms.

The fact that my cousin can watch this show multiple times amazes me. I'm not gonna lie and say that I'm not semi-interested in the outcome now that I've followed these women and their slow-talking Texan bachelor for an entire season's worth of episodes, but I certainly won't be watching the show *again* once I already know who "wins."

There's a knock and the door swings open. Penny hits PAUSE so we don't miss a minute of the pre-rose-ceremony limo confessions.

"Hey, ladies." Russ walks in, wearing a tight green shirt and dirty-looking jeans. I turn back to the TV.

"Scooch," he says, moving me from my comfortable corner spot on the couch—excuse me, my *bed*—and into the crowded center. "What are we watching?"

"Season eleven," says Penny.

"I hear this is a good one!" says Russ, slapping my leg. I look up at him with a sneer, but he smiles back at me. "I can tell this is your kind of show, Priscilla."

I'm in such a bad mood about Sebastian not calling that I'm not sure I can deal with Russ's infuriating behavior tonight. I fold my arms over my chest and stare at the TV.

Ten minutes later, Brad-the-Texan breaks up with both bachelorettes. "What a crock!" I shout.

"Seriously!" says Russ. "What the H?"

I've noticed with some amusement that Russ never curses. He even uses a euphemism for H-E-L-L.

"You guys!" shouts Penny, ready to defend her favorite show. "He was honest! He didn't find true love and so he couldn't commit to anyone. It was very noble."

"Bull," says Russ, again censoring himself. "You go on the show, you propose. Rules are rules."

"Agreed," I say.

"Well, that's a surprising word coming out of your mouth," says Russ, knocking me on the shoulder.

I shrug. When he's right, he's right.

"So, do you ladies want to go out tonight?"

he asks. "Cornflower Blue is playing at the Cactus."

"Let's go!" says Penny, pushing Miss Tiara off her lap.

"We're in our pajamas," I say grumpily. I don't know Cornflower Blue but they sound like an old country band.

"Oh, Quinn, snap out of your funk," says Penny, ruffling my hair as she walks behind the couch and upstairs to change into a sorority shirt and a tight skirt, no doubt.

"Is there a reason why you're especially moody tonight?" asks Russ.

"No," I say, picking at the blanket that's across my lap.

"Is something up with your friend the DJ?" he asks.

"No!" I shout, throwing off the blanket and standing up.

"Good!" he says. "So put on some clothes and let's go have fun."

I don't want to go, but I don't see a way to get out of it now. I stomp to the downstairs half bathroom and slide on my jean shorts. Then I slip a bra under my pajama T-shirt and run my fingers through my hair. I may go out, but I'm sure as H not going to try too hard if I'm just with Russ and Penny.

At the Cactus, I immediately realize I was right about the music. It's way country. But I stand in the crowd, just to show Russ that I'm open-minded. Even though *I hate country music.*

After the third song, I'm getting restless. That's when Russ leans over and whispers in my ear.

"This song is one that Fats Domino did in 1958," he says. "If you listen, you can hear the soul influence, too. Cornflower Blue does it really differently, but it's iconic."

"Hmm," I say, listening more to the lyrics and realizing that I do recognize the words a little.

The leaning-over-to-whisper thing keeps happening. As each song plays, Russ feels the need to give me some context. I don't really mind—it makes the music more bearable.

The last song the band plays is "Can't Help Falling in Love." UB40 did a cover of it in the nineties, but I know it's originally an Elvis song.

When Russ leans over to give me another history lesson, I turn to face him. "This one I know," I say.

"I'm glad to hear that," he says. "And as a reward for having such in-depth musical knowledge of a song that everyone in the world should be familiar with . . . may I have this dance?"

"Hmm, let me think. Insulting me and then asking me to dance . . ." I say, narrowing my eyes at his smug face. "No." I turn my back to him.

He taps my shoulder. "Pretty please, Priscilla?" he asks, holding out his arms.

"No way," I say.

"Quinn?" he asks.

Against my better judgment, I turn to him. The smugness is gone, and he has a look of sincere hope. I feel my heart melt a tiny bit.

"Oh, fine," I say.

When I give in, Russ instantly envelops me with his arms, which feel even stronger than they look. He actually knows how to dance—it's like we're doing some ballroom steps or something, and the way he puts pressure on my back helps me know where to move and how to stay in step with him. I feel like we're gliding.

"You're good," I say, looking up at him.

"When I'm dancing with the right person," he says, smiling back.

I blush. I actually *blush*. What is up with me tonight? And how is it that Russ, who always makes me feel slightly off balance, is suddenly making me feel perfectly at ease?

Chapter 10

I wake up Wednesday morning determined to change my profile playlist and take down the snapshot of me and Sebastian. Until I check my phone. There's a text from him that says, **Mother's tonight?**

I have to ask Penny to find out that he doesn't want me to meet his parents—Mother's is this legendary vegetarian spot. It's like guys have this sixth sense about when you're about to erase them from your life, and they just keep you holding on.

Pick me up at 7, I text back to him, along with Penny's address.

Then I lie down on my pillow and stare up at the ceiling. Last night when I got home, I downloaded that song—"Can't Help Falling in Love." It's an old song, but it sounds nice in a southern twang like the band had last night. Cornflower Blue sang it a little more quickly than the Elvis version, and that made dancing to it kind of fun. I smile to myself and sigh as I put in my headphones to listen to it—just once—before I start my day.

After one—okay, two—listens, I get up to dress and take Miss Tiara for a quick walk around the condo complex. She doesn't like going very far, which is convenient since being out in the five-hundred-degree weather doesn't agree with me either. It looks like it's going to rain today, though, which might cool things off. Just as I get back to the door, the sky opens up and it starts to pour.

I stumble inside quickly, holding Miss Tiara under my arm so a drop doesn't touch her—she's incredibly particular about getting wet. Penny says she insists on bubble baths, and somehow I believe that. I've come to accept the myths of Miss Tiara's life without question.

I look up and see that Chrissy is sitting in the living room holding the DVD of *Made of Honor*.

"Patrick Dempsey in a wedding mooovie,"

she says in a singsong voice. "I doubt there could be anything better for a rainy summer day."

I've found lots of ways to occupy my Tuesday-through-Friday lulls—driving through town, meeting up with Jade for lunch from the taco truck, sitting on campus and dreaming about college, reading (four books so far, thank you very much!)—but watching romantic comedies with Chrissy isn't high on my list. She tends to do it at least three afternoons a week. I hesitate, but this Patrick Dempsey vehicle is a new one, at least.

"I'll pop some popcorn," I say, heading into the kitchen to hunt for Orville Redenbacher.

Chrissy fascinates me. She's your typical sorority girl, but she really *is* that way. I guess I always thought the giddiness, the bubbly behavior, and the never-ending concern about boob saggage were fake, but Chrissy is as genuine as I am. She's just a different person. I notice that her legs are all banged up under her skirt, and I almost ask her about the bruises, but I don't want to seem nosy. Still, I get the feeling there's a lot I don't know about her. By the end of the movie she's crying with happy tears and

I'm crying with tears of relief that it's over.

Okay, I'm not really crying. But she is. And I'm truly glad we're done here.

"That was *sooo* sweet," she says, sniffling.

"Yes, and totally unpredictable," I say sarcastically.

She nods earnestly and grabs a tissue from the coffee table to blow her nose. When she asks if I want to watch *Bridget Jones's Diary* (again), I tell her I have some work to do and go upstairs to Miss Tiara's room with my laptop. As I stalk people from my high school on Facebook, the sound of Chrissy's laughter at Renee Zellweger's über-hilarious antics echoes downstairs.

By the time seven o'clock rolls around, I'm so ready for Sebastian's double-honk, and I finally hear it outside. Not that I'm going to let him off the hook easily—he deserves some chastising.

I swing a leg over the back of the Vespa, and feel a thrill rush through me. It's a moment when I'm allowed to be close to him, to pull his lanky frame into me and lean my head on his shoulder. I intend to enjoy it.

As we park at Mother's, I force myself back

into slightly mad mode. I get off the bike and shake my hair out, seductively but distantly. I'm still upset that he didn't call when he said he would. And that doesn't make me a bachelorette, just someone who appreciates an honest guy.

At our corner table, the over-iced waters have already left little pools of wetness. I push a napkin under my glass and concentrate on soaking it up.

"I did this great show on Sunday," says Sebastian excitedly. He starts to arrange the salt and pepper shakers on the edge of the table.

"Let's say this is the DJ booth and it's, like, five feet higher than the dance floor." He moves his place mat to the center of the table to represent the dance floor.

"There were tons of people and it was like I was above them," he says. "I was handing down musical knowledge."

"Cool," I say, sipping my chilly water.

When the server comes to take our order, Sebastian is in the middle of his "here's what I played" rant, and he shoos her away with his hand without looking up.

"Sorry," I say to her. "Can we have five more minutes?"

She smiles and walks back to the kitchen.

Sebastian pauses his story, but he looks annoyed.

"Are you mad or something?" he asks, suddenly tuning into me. "You're not even listening."

"You didn't call," I say. I believe in being direct about these things.

"I texted you this morning," he says.

"You said 'over the weekend,'" I remind him, feeling frustrated with myself for sounding like a nag. But really, when a person says he'll call after a kiss like that, you expect him to *call*. I even considered opening Penny's copy of *He's Just Not That Into You* on Sunday night, but thankfully, I restrained myself.

"I had shows," says Sebastian. "I didn't mean to let you down or anything."

I glance up and see his sexy dark hair fall over his eyes. He looks sorry.

"It's okay," I say. "It's not a big deal." It isn't, right? I'm just being needy. It must be the Tri-Pi vibes at the condo getting to me. I am cool, I am not going to be nitpicky about when he calls. So

I encourage him to go on. "Tell me more about your show," I say.

And he does. He shares the set list, the influences he considered mixing, the still-unreleased Long Armed Stapler album he worked on, how he spun Pauper Palace, the Flaming Squirrels, and Courtship in a gloriously underground compilation that finished off with "Love That Red" by Art Girls Gone Bad.

After dinner, we hit an outdoor venue, where the band is set up next to a rickety picket fence, and we keep talking songs. Sebastian tells me that country music isn't all bad—just mostly—and I tell him about the Top 40 world, which claims the lives of great indie bands all too often.

"I hate hearing silly girls prattle on about how much they love one of my favorite underground bands after they hear *one song* on an episode of some lame CW series," I say.

He nods in agreement. "Right on."

Sebastian hasn't ever listened to Top 40, he says, and he doesn't even own a TV. Which is probably why he doesn't get it when I describe the girl in front of us as "someone you'd see on

The Bachelor." But I don't mind.

I love listening to him, and this is the type of indie-music-nerd conversation I've dreamed of having with someone other than Raina. . . . With a hot guy, perhaps. And here he is. Right in front of me.

When he hits the bathroom, though, I realize I'm humming to myself. *Ugh!* Why can't I get "Can't Help Falling in Love" out of my mind? I blame it on my lack of iron today—next time I'll ask Sebastian to take me to a place that serves both steak *and* tofu.

When he drops me off at home after midnight, we share a long kiss, and I imagine how cool we must look, making out on a Vespa in the moonlight. Who cares what Russ said? I love this Euro bike. When I get inside, I sneak into the half bathroom and dial Raina. I don't want to wake up Penny, because I remember that she has some crazy bonding excursion with sorority members—sorry, *sisters*—early tomorrow morning. A ropes course or a trust-fall trip or something like that. Is it bad that I only half listen to her?

"Raina," I loud-whisper. "Sebastian just left."

"And?" she squeals excitedly, not unlike the girls on *The Bachelor*.

"He's brilliant," I say. "He knows everything about music—tons of songs that I don't even know yet but can't wait to download—he took me to a fantastic outdoor show tonight by this band called The Page Jumpers, and he seems really into me."

"How are the kisses?" she asks, getting right down to business. "Still hot?"

"Yes," I say, thinking about the ten-minute make-out session we had outside the condo. "Too bad Miss Tiara would crowd my sleepover!"

We both laugh. "It sounds so perfect, Quinn," says Raina. "Is there anything remotely unperfect about your summer?"

"Just Penny's sorority obsession," I say. "Oh, and this neighbor cowboy-wannabe who thinks he's really cool. He won't stop calling me Priscilla."

"Drag," says Raina. "But still, deal-able if you've got Sebastian to play with."

I laugh. "What's going on there?" I ask, not wanting to be that self-involved friend.

"I'm just stuck working at the movie theater

and wishing they'd change the 'I Love 1983' CD," says Raina.

"Hey, that CD has Toto on it," I say, half jokingly. "Don't knock it!"

"You're right," she says. "'Africa' is a classic song. Oh, and there's this new guy who started, but he's nerd city. Nasal and slouchy and way into science fiction."

"Sounds like a dream," I say.

"You're the one living the dream," says Raina. "But I'll be here when you get back to reality."

"Thanks," I say.

When we hang up, I crawl into bed and open my laptop. I feel like downloading some songs that Sebastian mentioned tonight. I search for Art Girls Gone Bad, Rainbow Forks, and Blue Solar System and listen to a few tracks, adding the ones that I really like to my iPod.

And then, just before I go to bed, I download Elvis's "Can't Help Falling in Love," just to compliment the Cornflower Blue version that I heard last night. I fall asleep with that song in my ears.

Chapter 11

I'm half awake, dreaming of coffee. More specifically, the smell of coffee. And Russ's voice. Humming. I must have listened to that Elvis song one too many times last night. I slowly open my eyes and pull the one still-in-place earbud out of my ear.

"Daa-daa-daaa . . . da-da-da-daaa-daaa . . ." I still hear that nonsensical tune. I sit up, grouchy. It feels early, but when I look at the clock I see it's eleven A.M. There's more noise from the kitchen.

"Penny?" I call out. She must have left a couple of hours ago for that sorority-bonding thing. Unless it's raining. I lean over the couch to peek out the deck doors. Nope. Sunny and hot. Surprise.

"Priscilla, are you finally up?" Russ walks into the living room—my bedroom—with a steaming cup of coffee.

I scramble to make sure my legs are covered. I'm a T-shirt-and-underwear girl at bedtime.

"What are you doing here?!" I say, mustering as much indignation as I can for a just-waking moment.

"I finished my paper," he says. "I turned it in this morning, and I am officially a rising senior. I'm in the mood to celebrate."

"Do frat boys always celebrate by scaring sleeping girls?" I ask. "Wait. Don't answer that."

"Be nice if you want your coffee," he says, pulling the mug away from me.

"Okay," I say, reaching out for it. "Thank you." I've never been a huge coffee person, but I have to admit it smells really good this morning.

Russ hands me the mug and sits down in the corner chair. "So, Priscilla," he says. "What are we doing today?"

I take a sip of the coffee—it *is* good—and look up at him. I'm contemplating shutting him down and saying that *we* are not doing anything, but the truth is that I don't have plans. And I'm bored.

"It's your town," I challenge. "You tell me."

"Barton Springs," he says.

And before I can ask him what that means, he jumps up and heads out the door. "Get on your bathing suit!" he shouts just before the door closes.

I carefully put down my coffee mug and wait for his overenthusiastic butt to return. In the meantime, I grab my jean shorts and put them on with the oversized Sixty3 concert tee that I like to wear to bed. Two minutes later, Russ is back.

"Didn't you hear me?" he asks. "Barton Springs—let's go!"

"First of all," I say, picking up my coffee mug for another sip, "I have no idea what 'Barton Springs' means. And second, I didn't bring a bathing suit." I'm not the poolside type—and I burn really easily.

"Borrow one from Penny," he says, undeterred. "You will love this spot. It's an old natural spring and it's constantly sixty-eight degrees, so it feels warm in the winter and cool in the summer. Plus, you get to lie out on a hill of mowed grass instead of sand. Somehow I don't think you're a sandy-beach girl."

"You got that right," I say, not moving.

"Come on, Priscilla!" he says, leaning down and resting his head on the back of the couch sideways to give me puppy-dog eyes. "It'll be fun. You can bring your iPod and tune me out if you want."

I smile. Swimming in cool water does sound nice. I haven't dealt with this much heat since summer camp five years ago, when I was a counselor in training at a sailing camp on the Neuse River in North Carolina. We had an insane heat wave and everyone had to sleep with, like, four fans pointed at them just to endure it. The only relief was swimming in the pondlike pool—it was packed every day. But that water did feel good. There's something about splashing around on hundred-degree days.

"Give me three minutes," I say, standing and heading upstairs to Penny's room.

Miss Tiara eyes me suspiciously as I poke through my cousin's drawers. I find six—yes, *six*—teensy bikinis, but nothing with a remotely reasonable amount of coverage. I choose an orange-and-white polka-dot suit with a ruffle around the bottom. It's the one with the most fabric. When I put it on, Miss Tiara growls.

"I don't have another option, picky priss!" I whisper at her. I pull on my jean shorts and Sixty3 tee over the suit. This will have to do. I grab a towel from the bathroom and meet Russ downstairs, making sure to pick up my iPod.

I offer to drive but he just looks at my yellow Festiva in the parking lot and laughs. "Let's take the truck," he says.

"If you want to waste gas . . ." I say, annoyed.

"I'm all for saving face by losing gas," he says, opening the passenger-side door for me. "If anyone I know is at the Springs, I cannot be seen climbing out of that clown car."

I step into the truck and feel the hot and squishy vinyl seat, so I put down my towel to sit on. I don't need my thighs to get stuck in their own sweat.

Russ shuts the door behind me.

I give him a *hmph* and roll down the truck window. I wish one of our cars, at least, had AC. By the time we get to Barton Springs, I'm dripping with sweat and I realize that in the rush to find a slightly modest bathing suit, I forgot to protect my pasty white skin.

"Do you have any sunblock?" I ask Russ as we pull into a parking spot.

He hops out and grabs a giant canvas bag from the back bed. On top of his towel is a bottle of Coppertone that looks like it's twenty years old.

I eye it warily.

"It's all I got, Priscilla," he says. "Take it or leave it."

He's waving the bottle in front of me teasingly. I snatch it.

"Nice snag," he says, closing his eyes and turning his face toward the sun. "Me, I'm gonna get a little tan today."

I look at Russ's face. His strong jawline moves up and down as he chews a piece of gum, and his rust-colored hair is getting longer, I notice. It's curling over his ear a little and almost touching the back of his plaid collar. He cut off the arms of the shirt, and the tan on his biceps looks golden enough to me.

"Ready?" he asks, clapping his hands together.

I'm a little startled to see him snap his eyes open and look at me looking at him. *Did he know*

I was looking at him? I mean, obviously he knew I was looking, but did he know I was *looking* looking? I have really dark aviator sunglasses on, so he probably can't tell where my eyes are, right?

"You should really wear sunblock," I say snarkily to hide my embarrassment. "You could die of skin cancer."

We pay a small admission fee and enter alongside what looks like a really long, narrow swimming pool. The springs are blocked off partially by a dam at one end, and Russ and I walk that way to cross over to the far side, which is grassy. He leads me to a huge pecan tree.

"Shade for you, sun for me," he says, pulling a blue cotton blanket out of the huge bag he brought.

I spread out my piddly off-white bath towel.

"There's room on mine," he says, laying half of his blanket in the shade.

"That's okay," I say. "I'm fine over here."

I put my towel on the far side of his blanket, well in the shade, so that there's a good four feet between us. I sit down and slather sunblock on my arms, hands, calves, feet, and face, which are the only parts that are exposed right now—I'm not ready for the bikini reveal. I start to click through my iPod, trying to find the right album for the day.

Then Russ takes off his shirt, and I lose my mind. I've never been one of those girls who goes gaga for muscles. I never tore out a teen magazine centerfold for my locker—I was more likely to put up *Venus Zine* interviews. I never got the appeal of Nick Lachey when there were guys like Jack White who deserved my attention. But up close and in person, let me just say that *muscles look good*.

"Do you really think I need sunblock?" asks Russ, squinting at me.

I will my eyes to move up from his abs, thanking God again for sunglasses.

"Yeah, I do," I say, handing over the bottle.

I lie back on my little towel and concentrate on a good iPod selection, willing my head not to turn to the left, willing my eyes not to be drawn to the way his hands are moving over his undeniably beautiful body.

"A little help?" He laughs, breaking my do-not-stare concentration.

"Huh?" I ask, looking over and focusing my eyes on his face, just his face.

"I can't reach my back," he says.

I feel like I'm in the middle of a horribly awkward movie scene. I take the sunblock from him and scoot over onto the shady side of his blanket. After I pour the lotion into my hand, I close my eyes and start to spread it over his back. My heartbeat speeds up as my hands touch his skin, and I hope he can't feel my freakishly fast pulse. I do a really shoddy job, honestly, because I'm eager to stop and slow down my racing heart.

"Done!" I say overly cheerful, wiping the extra lotion on my legs. Then I slide back to my towel, press PLAY, and lie down with my eyes closed.

Within three minutes, I'm so hot I might scream. I sit up on my elbows and look at everyone splashing in the water, running around in next to nothing. I guess my bikini will fit in here.

Slowly, I unbutton my jeans and pull them off my pale legs. Then I slip off my T-shirt.

"Hook 'em, Horns!" shouts Russ. "Wooooo-hoooo!"

"Excuse me?" I ask, hoping he's not making some crude reference to my body, which I'm comfortable with, but not, like, confident about. Is anyone really one hundred percent sure of herself in a bathing suit? I mean, besides Olympic swimmers. *Did he say "Horns"?*

"That's a UT bikini—burnt-orange and white!" Russ says. Then he whistles in appreciation.

"I had no idea," I say.

"Well, it was a good choice," Russ says, smiling at me. I wish he would quit looking over here. I lie back down.

"Let's go in the water!" he says. And it's one of those requests that's not really a question—it's a demand. Like the neighbor boys who used to spray me with Super Soakers in my front yard, Russ will take no prisoners. Because I don't feel like being dragged into the spring, I willingly stand up and saunter to the concrete edge behind him.

He jumps in, shaking his head with a "brrr" when he surfaces. I can't imagine being cold right now in this hundred-degree heat, but the idea is appealing. I spring off the side and into the water.

Ice cubes. Penguins. Klondike bars. It is *freezing*. And awesome. I give Russ a toothy grin—I can't help myself. He swims over to me and we tread water next to each other; neither of us can stand in this deep end.

"I'm impressed," he says. "I thought you'd take major coaxing to get in."

"You don't really know me very well," I say, swimming to the wall so I can hold on and rest for a minute. I'm often the first person to jump in a pool, ever since I figured out that the last person in is always the one who gets teased and splashed the most.

Russ follows me to the wall. "I know you a little, Priscilla," he says, grabbing the side ladder.

"A very little," I say. "Just because you insist on using my real first name doesn't mean you know me."

Russ climbs up the ladder and sits on the edge of the pool next to where I'm holding the side. "I know you like The Walters, you're obsessed with your iPod, you're a creature of shade, and you're into skinny-ass DJs," says Russ with a self-satisfied smile. "What do you know about me?"

I push off from the side and swim out in front of him, turning to face him. "I know that you're cocky about your car and your muscles, you're a complete frat boy, you *think* you're really smart and mature, you procrastinate like crazy with your work, you're irresponsible about sunscreen, and you like burgers."

"I don't think I'm so smart," says Russ, his half smile giving away that he *does too*!

"Wanna race?" I ask.

"What'd you say?" says Russ, standing up.

"You heard me," I say. "Go!"

I start swimming my ass off to the other side of the spring, which is a good hundred feet at least, and I can hear Russ splash in behind me and start booking it. He beats me by a solid three seconds, despite my head start, but I'm laughing and out of breath when I reach the wall. I'm glad he didn't let me win.

"Okay," says Russ, who seems irritatingly unfazed by our burst of physical activity. "Tell me more about yourself."

"I can't just start telling you things," I say, breathing hard. "I don't know what to say."

"Tell me one thing, right now, that I don't know about you," he says.

"I like strawberry milk shakes better than chocolate or vanilla," I say. Then I duck under the water and smooth down my hair.

"I prefer coffee milk shakes," Russ says when I surface.

"Fall is my favorite season," I say. "Especially where my grandpa lives in Connecticut, when the leaves turn into flames of color."

"I like bluebonnets in the spring down here," Russ counters.

"The best barbecue in Carolina is at Allen and Son," I say.

"Here, it's a place called Iron Works," says Russ.

"I love the way American cheese melts," I say. "It's superior to all other cheeses in any dish that calls for melting."

"I sometimes prefer Swiss," says Russ. "I like the sharp bite."

He winks at me. I roll my eyes and continue.

"I once knew this girl who worked at my

movie theater who went to New York and became a famous model," I say.

"I once got to play guitar while Daniel Johnston sang," he says.

"No way!" I gasp.

"Yes way," he says. "He was at this café where I was hanging out and strumming, and he just came up and sang a little while I leaned back and played. It was very cool."

"That's amazing," I say. "Better than my model story."

"It's not a competition," says Russ, splashing me. "Keep going."

"My favorite book-to-movie adaptation is *The Last Picture Show*," I say, trying to sound smart and film-knowledgeable by referencing this old seventies movie, set in small-town Texas.

"Cybill Shepherd rules," he says, showing that he knows the movie too.

I laugh, and Russ cocks his head sideways at me.

"You know, when you smile I just want to kiss you," he says.

My eyes widen in surprise and I hurriedly turn around, swimming for the other side.

Russ laughs. "Are we racing again?!" he shouts after me. But I don't answer, I just freestyle like my life depends on it.

I hightail it out of the spring and back up to land, afraid to look at Russ. How *weird* of him to say that to me! I'm half mad and half scared and half—I don't know—confused. That's three halves, but you get what I'm saying.

Just as I lay down and put on my iPod to calm my emotions, I feel a tap on my shoulder. I pull out an earbud and look up to see Russ leaning over me.

"I'm sorry I said that," he says, "about the kiss."

"Okay," I say, not sure how to respond.

"I meant it," he says softly, his face hovering just inches above mine. He pauses for a moment there and I stare up at his big blue eyes.

Two beats later, he pulls back, sits up, and says, "But I'm sorry I said it."

I force my lips into a tight grin as I sit up on my elbows. "It's okay," I say. "No big deal."

He looks over his right shoulder at me, studying my face.

"It's just that I'm kind of with someone

already this summer," I say. I did *not* think I'd have to be having this conversation with a Texas frat cowboy. Can't he see how different we are?

"The skinny-ass DJ," says Russ.

"Sebastian," I say.

"Whatever," he says, shrugging, and then he stands up and heads back to the water. I feel bad, but what am I supposed to tell him?

An hour later, I'm sitting in the shade under the tree, safely on my towel, when Russ comes back out of the water after more major lap swim-mage.

He smiles brightly, looking totally over everything. "You ready?" he asks.

"For what?" I ask.

"The bats!" he says, shaking his head out so droplets of water rain down on me.

"Huh?" I ask. I'm really not in the mood for baseball in this heat.

Russ shakes his head, laughing. "Priscilla, you have a lot left to see in Austin that your one-track DJ isn't going to show you," he says. "Let's go."

When Russ parks the truck in the parking lot of the Four Seasons Hotel, I give him a skeptical eye. He grabs an old umbrella out of the back cab, confusing me further. The sky is crystal clear.

"Trust me," he says. We walk into the hotel, and I feel sheepish in my wet-spotted T-shirt and shorts, but Russ just strolls through as if he owns the place. He points out a flag in the lobby that was flown in 1835 in the town of Gonzales, Texas, as a warning to the Mexican forces who had instructions to confiscate the cannon, according to the plaque. It has a cannon on it, and it reads, COME AND TAKE IT.

"Yikes," I say.

"Baddest-ass flag ever," says Russ. Then he keeps walking through the hotel doors and we head down a sloping lawn to an area with a few chairs that face the water.

"This is Town Lake," says Russ. "And that's the Congress Avenue Bridge." He points to our right. Then he starts to say the weirdest things.

"So, there are probably a million bats under that bridge right now," says Russ.

"You mean like flying minions of Dracula?" I ask. "That kind of bat?"

"I wouldn't bring vampires into this," says

Russ. "But yes, that kind of bat."

"I'm intrigued," I admit. "Go on."

"Well, at sunset, they all come out to look for food," he says. "They stream over the water and fill the sky with black wings. It's incredible! It's like this giant cloud of creatures hovering over you."

Russ's eyes are lit up like he's telling me we're about to win the lottery. His smile is wide open and his enthusiasm is infectious.

"That sounds amazing," I say, sitting down in a chair next to him. "This is happening tonight?"

"Summer sunsets," he says. "That's when they're here. The bats are up from Mexico."

"Ooh, *murciélagos*," I say. For some reason the Spanish word for *bat* is one of the only things that has stuck in my head since eighth grade Spanish II.

"*Sí*, dork," says Russ.

"And the umbrella?" I ask, ignoring his jab.

"Well, it's not for rain," he says. "The sky is about to fill with mammals, Priscilla! You do the math."

"*Ewww!*" I wail, tucking my feet underneath

me in my wide wooden chair.

A waiter comes by to get us drinks from the bar, and Russ orders a root beer. It sounds so good, I get one too.

When they come, they're extra cold and frothy.

"Good choice," I say.

"Cheers," says Russ, clinking his mug with mine.

An older couple wanders down the lawn and joins us, sitting on the bench to our left. They're holding hands, I notice, which I always think is really annoying among people my age, but somehow sweet between couples like my parents' age and older. Maybe that's because my parents never hold hands. They love each other and all, but they just don't show it that way. This couple, though, is more like my grandparents' age.

"You two waiting for the bats?" asks the husband.

"Yes, sir," says Russ. "It'll be the first time for Priscilla here."

"We watched last night, but they didn't show," says the wife, looking at me.

I glance over at Russ.

"It's not a sure thing," he says. "But I thought it'd be fun to try."

"I guess bats are fickle," I say, looking back at the old couple.

"The concierge at the hotel says the bats are still pregnant and might not be ready to come out and feed yet," says the husband.

The way he says "feed" sounds a little gross to me, but I'm curious to see this bat phenomenon. We sit silently for a few more minutes, and Russ and I sip our root beers.

Even without the bats flying, this time around day's end is stunning. There is a brief golden moment that seems like it comes straight out of a cinematographer's filmic dream—the sparkling glow on the water, the bright green of the grass under the rose-hued sky. And Russ's hair with a shimmer of sundown in it. It's like a song.

"Are you disappointed?" he asks me, when the sun sets and we're left in the blue glow of twilight, sans flying rodents.

"No," I say. "It was lovely."

Chapter 12

On Friday night, I have plans to meet Jade and Sebastian at Dirty's. I go to Jade's house first to pick her up—she doesn't live too far from the Drag, which is this main strip near campus, and it's definitely my turn to drive.

When she gets in the Festiva, Jade instantly comments on the music. I realize I've been playing Russ's dusty-ass tape for days. I'm kind of into it.

"Old-school!" she says, when some insanely ancient Green Day song comes on.

"I think this is Russ's older brother's high school mix tape or something," I say.

"The family can't be all bad if he was into Billy Joe back in the day," says Jade.

By the time we get to Dirty's, Sebastian

is already spinning, and Jade and I grab two sodas and settle into our regular booth.

"I tried to see the bats this week," I say.

"It's early," she says. "They're probably still pregnant."

Funny how the bats are this normal thing to talk about in Austin. It's like I just said, "Oh, I went to the supermarket today." But I'm talking about flying mice here.

"Yeah, Russ took me down to the lawn by the Four Seasons and we were just—" I start.

"Wait," interrupts Jade. "You went on a date with your fratty neighbor? *And* you have his mix tape playing in your car . . . ?"

"It was *not* a date," I say firmly. "More like I was looking for something to do. That's all."

"You must have been really bored," says Jade, taking a sip of her drink and looking back toward Sebastian.

"Russ isn't that bad," I say.

"He's not?" she asks. "You're always acting like he's the biggest a-hole on the planet with the way he won't call you 'Quinn' and how he hangs around all the time."

"Yeah," I say. "That's true. He does irritate me."

"Good thing you have Sebastian to focus on," says Jade, smiling.

I look over and see his fast hands replacing the Fretless Coma album that just played. Sebastian really is hot.

I hear the bells over the door jingle.

"Hey, there's Rick," I say to Jade, whose back is to the entrance. She doesn't turn around.

"Rick!" I shout, waving at him.

He looks at me for a minute, like he's trying to decide whether to come over. Does he think he's too cool to sit at a table with interns? He's always so nice at the Amalgam office.

"Hey, Quinn," he says, when he finally graces us with his presence. "Hey there, Jade."

She gives a barely audible "hi," still not looking up.

"Sit down," I say to Rick, scooting over in the booth. It's bizarre to see your boss out. It's kind of like seeing a teacher in the drugstore, when you realize that he is a person who has a life outside of your classroom, and maybe he's even wearing normal clothes or laughing with his wife or something. It's all very humanizing. And seeing Rick out is, of course, way cooler than seeing a teacher, because he's an amazing indie-record-label boss. So I really hope he sits down.

But he doesn't.

"I'm here to check out a band that's on after Sebastian," says Rick, looking only at me and not at Jade, I notice. She has her eyes down slightly. "I've got friends coming, so I'm just gonna wait at the bar."

And then, even though I know he's my boss and I really shouldn't talk back or question him or whatever, it has to be said:

"You guys are being weird," I say. "Did Jade get fired or something?"

I'm just joking but my comment is met with Silence.

Jade's head lowers like the top of the table is the most interesting thing she's ever seen in her life.

"You guys have a good night, okay?" says Rick, backing away. "I see my friends over there, so . . ."

"Dude, what the eff?" I ask Jade after Rick

is out of earshot. I smile inwardly at the fact that I self-censored my language, just like Russ did the other day.

But when I see Jade raise her head, I realize this is something serious. Her mascara is streaked in canals down her cheeks, and her bright red mouth is curved into an unnatural shape of angst.

"Oh my God," I say. "You *did* get fired."

"It's not that," says Jade, reaching for a tissue in her black canvas bag. Her voice is one of those jagged whispers that only crying people do well. She puts the tissue over her nose and blows.

"I looked up to Pitt," she says.

"Huh?" I ask. "Looked up to Pitt? You mean Brad? I guess he's *kind of* a role model, but I don't think he's anyone to get obsessed with. He's old, and he cheated on Jennifer Aniston." *Why do I know this stuff?*

Jade lowers the tissue and looks me dead in the eye.

"*I hooked up with Rick,*" she says, slowly and clearly.

"Oh," I say. *Ooooooh*. This is bad. "Is that legal?" I ask.

"Yes!" she snaps. "I'm eighteen."

Okay, okay, I guess that wasn't the best question I could have asked. But I'm not sure what to say here.

"Do you guys like each other?" I ask, trying again.

"Well, *I* like him!" she says, shredding, piece by piece, the poor, wet tissue as she stares down at the table. "Is he looking at us?"

I glance over her shoulder at the bar, where Rick is sitting on a stool and slapping the back of some overweight guy with a leather jacket and a buzz cut.

"No," I say, not sure if that's what Jade wants to hear.

She rips the tissue in half violently.

Over the next twenty minutes, I'm able to glean through sniffling tones that Jade has always had a crush on Rick, and that being in the office together this summer was part of her seduction plan. They had been flirting constantly and hanging out sometimes after work. Which explains why Jade never wanted to talk about her own love life, and never called me to do anything during the week. And then last night it came to a head. She and Rick hooked up in the demo closet.

"That actually sounds kind of amazing," I say. I'm picturing me with a guy in the Amalgam closet, listening to the Walters' still-unreleased album over the stereo while I prop my leg up on a mid-level shelf and get hot and heavy among the indie rock.

"It was," says Jade, looking at me with intense eyes and bringing me out of my fantasy. "Until he broke away from me and told me he thinks I'm hot but that I'm just a kid."

"Ouch," I say. "He said 'just a kid'? Those words? That's like a lame sitcom diss."

"Yeah," says Jade. "It's the worst. I called in sick today and I don't know if I can go back."

"I'll be there for you Monday," I say. "You have to show him that you don't care. That you're young and smoking and can get anyone you want."

"You think?" she asks.

"Of course!" I say. "He's lucky you turned those sexy brown eyes his way for a moment, but if he isn't smitten, he's forgotten."

I sound like one of Penny's self-help relationship books. But it seems like the right thing to say, because Jade is perking up.

"That's pretty harsh," says Jade, her voice finally losing that crying edge. "I don't know if I can turn my feelings around like that. I just always thought he was my ideal. I mean, he's the head of Amalgam Records, the guy who knows everyone in town, who has so much power and is still such a great person."

"It also doesn't hurt that he's pretty hot for a near-thirty-year-old," I say.

She smiles. "That's true too."

"You don't have to turn off your feelings," I say. "You just have to be the intern. Go to work, be your professional self, then leave. You'll find another guy—a much more ideal summer fling fit."

"Like you and Sebastian?" she asks.

"Yeah," I say. But when I look over at him, although I know he's so beautiful and all, I don't feel totally excited. And then I realize that when I imagined the Amalgam closet make-out session, I didn't picture myself with Sebastian.

I shake my head to clear my weird thoughts.

Sebastian is exactly the guy I am looking for this summer. Then I refocus on Jade.

"Bright side?" I ask.

"Please," she says.

"Your mascara is streaked in this really great way that makes you look like a hardcore eighties album-cover girl," I say.

Jade sticks out her tongue and gives me the hard-rock hand sign.

"Thanks, Quinn," she says.

"Anytime," I say. "Hey, you wanna get out of here?"

"Yeah," she says. "But you stay—I know you want to meet up with Sebastian after his set. I can take the bus or something."

"It's okay," I say. "I kind of feel like going home myself."

When I get back to the condo, I call Raina but she doesn't pick up. Penny's not around, which would normally be a good thing, but I kind of feel like talking to someone right now.

I walk out onto the back deck to get some air, and I smell a delicious burger cooking. I look over at Russ and Chrissy's deck, which is connected to ours, and see that someone has the grill going. Then Russ walks outside with a spatula in his hand.

He's wearing a bright blue polo shirt that makes his eyes look even more unreal than usual. Of course, he has on khaki cargo shorts too. The guy is a walking frat stereotype. *So why can't I stop thinking about him?*

"What's up, Priscilla?" He smiles at me and cocks his head. "Date end early?"

"I was just out," I say. "It wasn't really a date or anything." Not that this is any of his business.

"Want a burger?" he asks.

Yes.

"Isn't it a weird time to be grilling?" I ask. "It's, like, midnight."

"I got hungry," he says. "And I have American cheese, which I know you can't resist." He points to the Velveeta slices on his picnic table. "Come on over."

We're divided by a small wooden barrier, so I walk down the three short steps off of Penny's deck and up the steps to his. The siren song of burgers with American cheese is too much for my weak carnivorous self to resist.

I sit down on the wooden bench and stare at the condiment tray Russ has brought out—it has ketchup, mustard, mayonnaise, dill pickles, sliced onions, lettuce, and tomatoes.

"You're a regular outdoor café over here," I say.

"I like grilling," says Russ. "And then I really like loading up a burger and eating."

I tuck my hair, which is slowly growing out and getting practically girl-length, behind my ears.

"So how come you aren't out?" I ask.

"I felt like taking it easy tonight," he says. "I was watching *Rocky* on TV, but then I got hungry, so . . ."

"Here we are," I say.

"Here we are," he says. He's looking at me and suddenly the grill starts shooting flames. A black cloud of smoke spits up, and Russ yells, "Dang! I hope you like 'em well done!" He's standing back from the grill and trying to use the long spatula to rescue the sad little burger that has just been charred to a crisp.

I clap my hand over my mouth, trying so

hard to hold in my laughter that I feel tears come to my eyes. Russ takes off his flip-flop and starts waving it around to clear the smoke. It only makes me laugh more.

"If you keep laughing, I'm gonna make you eat that one," says Russ, finally nabbing the burn-victim burger.

"I'm sorry," I say, still unable to hide my amusement. "You seemed like you were really good at all this until a minute ago."

"Yeah, well, you distracted me," says Russ, pretending to be huffy. He puts another two patties on the grill. "Let's try this again."

"Medium rare," I say.

"Yes, Queen Priscilla." He bows.

"So is Russ your real name?" I ask him, trying to turn the tables on this whole Priscilla thing.

"Yup," he says. "Russ Jay Barnes. Not Russell or Rusty or Russert. Just Russ. My parents are one-syllable folks."

"Oh," I say. "Then maybe you should understand that I'm a one-syllable girl, too. Quinn. Can you say it? *Quiiiiinnn*."

"Why do you fight your real name?" asks

Russ. "It fits you so perfectly."

"It does not!" I say. "It's old-fashioned, for one. And it's just so prissy. It even *sounds* like the word *prissy*. I am so not a Priscilla."

"That's where you're wrong," says Russ, turning back to the grill. "Priscilla is the rock-ingest name in the book."

He turns around with his lip curled up. "Come on, 'Cilla," he says.

I fight to keep from laughing again. "Is that the best Elvis you can do?" I deadpan.

"Wiiiise men say . . . only fools rush in . . ." He starts singing "Can't Help Falling in Love," which I now have about four versions of on my iPod. Then he comes around to my side of the picnic table and reaches for my hand.

And before I can figure out how to deter him, we're dancing on this silly condo deck at midnight to the sound of Russ's bad Elvis impersonation. I spin around a few times, trying to keep my head turned to the side, trying to figure out what it is that I'm feeling right now as my fingers lightly brush the back of his cotton polo shirt.

What am I doing? This guy is a jock-y goofball

134

with big muscles and a taste for country music.

"The burgers are gonna burn," I say after a minute.

Russ backs away from me and smiles.

"You're right, 'Cilla," he says, still doing Elvis. "We got a hunka hunka burning meat to attend to."

"Gross," I say. I sit back down at the table.

I try not to look up at him as I get my sesame-seed bun ready with condiments and toppings. I don't want him to think that I like him, or that he has a shot or whatever. He doesn't.

When I dig into the burger Russ cooked, I soften a little and smile. It's delicious, especially since he insisted I slather it with every condiment on the table. I tried to skip the mayo, but Russ insisted that a touch of it mixed with the ketchup was key. And he's not wrong.

"Mmm . . ." I say with a full mouth.

Russ looks at me and laughs, bringing a napkin up to my chin.

"Enjoying yourself, juice face?" he asks as he wipes my face like I'm five.

I put the burger down, slightly embarrassed.

"So what did happen tonight, anyway?"

Russ asks. "You seemed kind of upset when you came out on the deck earlier."

"Oh, nothing," I say. "My friend Jade is having guy issues, so we were talking about that and then I just didn't feel like staying out."

"So it was your *friend* having guy issues," says Russ. "Not you."

"No," I say defensively. "Not me. I'm into Sebastian. He's cool and really smart and he knows a ton about music."

Russ curls his lip again. "But can he do the King?" he asks.

I laugh. "What is it with you country boys and Elvis?" I ask. "The guy died decades before we were even born."

"It's not like I've got a shrine to Graceland in my room," says Russ. "But, you know, he was really influential on the stuff I listen to now—the same stuff you listen to now, too, by the way."

"He's okay," I say. "But he's kinda country. I just don't like that kind of music."

"Priscilla, are you gonna keep saying that kind of stupid thing all summer?" Russ asks. "I thought Austin would have opened your eyes a little by now."

I look at him, and I realize that he's being serious. He might even be a little bit annoyed with me.

"I'm seeing a lot of local bands," I say. "I mean, I've been going to shows with Jade and everything."

"I just hope you're going to more than Dirty's," says Russ. "Not that it's a bad venue, but you need to be getting all the flavor here."

"I know what I like," I say. "It's a certain type of music and I'm just not into stuff like bluegrass and banjos."

"Music is music, Priscilla," says Russ. "If you love music, you give it all a listen. You see what there is to learn in every song you hear. You take chances on shows. That's part of it."

"You think that manufactured pop count-down stuff is music?" I ask.

"Lots of your indie bands end up on those charts, let's not forget," says Russ.

"I know," I say bitterly. "And I hate that. I hate when annoying giggly girls know one song from a great band because it just happened to be on a movie soundtrack or something. They're totally co-opting the music and selling out the sound."

Russ laughs. "Do you hear yourself?" he asks. "You sound like a conspiracy theorist."

"It's true!" I say. "I loved 201 Bunnies Named Earl *way* before anyone else, and then one of their songs shows up in a cell phone commercial and now it's Penny's ringtone."

"For a smart girl, you sure say a lot of idiotic things," says Russ.

"What did you say to me?" I ask.

"It's true," he says. "Who cares about Penny's ringtone? If she likes the music, she likes the music. You don't own it. You can't tell people what to like—you can't control who likes the bands you like." He shakes his head. "Are you gonna go to college with that small-minded attitude?"

Then he stands up and turns his back to me. He starts cleaning the grill.

"I am *not* small-minded!" I shout, which is all I can think of to say even though I want to say something better, more biting.

I settle for standing up and marching down his stairs, then up mine. I get enough stomping in to communicate the fact that I feel insulted, but Russ doesn't look up from the grill.

"Thanks for the food," I say angrily, not understanding how Russ can take me from laughing and dancing to yelling and stomping in less then five minutes. "I only wish the conversation had been as good as the burger!" I shout, grasping for some sort of dig.

"You're welcome, Priscilla," Russ says calmly, not turning around.

Ooh, he makes me mad! I slide open the glass door, and if it weren't so heavy I'd have a mind to slam it, but I can't, so I just shut it tightly and flip the lock loudly so I'm sure Russ hears it and feels unwelcome in the condo. And that goes for my thoughts, too!

Chapter 13

The next morning, I wake up at eight A.M. without earbuds in my ears. I fell asleep in silence for the first time in a while. I hate that I let Russ get to me like that, but he made me feel like I don't know where I stand or what I like. I couldn't pick an album for my frustrated mood.

I check my phone and see a text from Sebastian that he sent around two A.M. "Where'd u go?" it asks. I text back, "Felt sick." Then I put the phone back on the coffee table. I can't deal right now.

It's really early, but I know I won't be able to fall asleep again, so I walk into the kitchen to make myself a fruit bowl—the breakfast of choice around here. I consider going outside on the deck to eat, because it might not be too hot at this hour, but I don't want to risk seeing

Russ. Miss Tiara pads downstairs, and I open the sliding door to let her out for a minute.

Then I notice that there's something leaning up against the glass. It's a CD case . . . and a cassette tape too. I peek around outside as I bend over to pick them up—no one in sight. I bring the gifts to the table and sit down to look them over—they're both a mix from Russ that he called "Indie + Country = Harmony." He made a CD and then copied it onto a tape for my car, I realize. It would be thoughtful if it weren't kind of presumptuous. I don't know if I want a mix from Russ.

I turn the CD cover over in my hand. Russ's writing is really messy. It's like boys are incapable of good penmanship because their hands are so energetic and spazzy. Not that my own writing was ever any good—but I'm having to work really hard to read this. I recognize half the song names, but the artists aren't ones I know. Then on the second half of the tape, there are some great bands doing songs I've never heard of. I realize that it must be country singers covering indie songs, and vice versa. A mix.

Way to be heavy-handed, I think, as I walk

over to the couch and open my laptop. When I click PLAY, I hear the familiar chords of a Sure Loser song, except it's being done in a different style. A style I've always been turned off by. It still doesn't sound great to me, but I'm going to prove Russ wrong. I *do* give music a chance, and I am going to sit here and listen to the whole thing, song by song. Even if I hate it. And I am *not* putting this mix on my iPod until I've heard at least a few songs. No need giving up precious memory to stuff I probably won't like.

I press PAUSE and make myself a cup of coffee, because I think I'll need it. Miss Tiara scratches at the door, so I let her back in and she jumps up on the couch to join me as I settle back into the cushions. Then I press PLAY.

By the third song, I'm getting into it. *Kind of*. I mean, I'm not a hundred percent into the way there's a male singer doing a Chihuahua Chicks song—it just seems wrong. When track six comes on, I have to admit that I'm hearing an excellent version of "Pretty in Black." I'm not saying it's better than the original, but it might be just as good. Not that I'd tell Russ that.

When Penny comes down for breakfast, I'm

on the last song—it's The Walters doing an old country tune called "Waltz Across Texas." And it's excellent. I may have to look up the original version.

"I thought you didn't like country music," Penny says sleepily as she walks past me and into the kitchen.

"I didn't," I say as I copy the mix onto my iPod.

I spend all of Saturday with the mix, and I even convince Penny to ride in my car when we make a pet store run to get Miss Tiara's special toothpaste so I can check out the cassette tape too. There's something about the voices—lilting and soft, then booming and angst-filled—that reminds me of what I love about indie rock. By the fourth play, I find myself humming along to the choruses—country style. I'm still not ready to say that these songs are new favorites, but I *am* surprised by them. They're not terrible.

When I wake up on Sunday morning, I feel like I have a music hangover. I reach over to the coffee table to pick up my phone, and I see a text from Jade. "Derby?" it says. I have no clue what she's talking about, but when I text her back I find out that she's proposing we go see some girls on roller skates kicking ass, which sounds okay to me. Jade tells me she just wanted a girls' day out, and I'm all for that after this weird, music-filled weekend.

She picks me up around eleven A.M. and we drive to a small stadium with a rink surrounded by banners that say TEXAS ROLLER-GIRLS. The teams have names like Texecutioners and Hotrod Honeys, and the women who are gearing up in pads and helmets are also dressed in amazing clothes—gingham shirts and denim skirts, or full-color jumpers. Some have braids in their hair, others wear striped knee socks.

"This is hot," I say to Jade as we take our seats near the edge of the rink.

"Wait till someone collides with you," says Jade. "You may go home with a black-eye souvenir."

I look at her and wonder if she's kidding, but she seems serious.

Jade explains to me that roller derby started in the 1930s, but kind of became a glitter-and-spandex fest in the eighties before it died out.

Then, a few years ago, a group of rocker girls in Austin decided to bring back the sport, complete with bands at the games.

"It's like a cross between a mosh pit and a burlesque show," she says.

"You know a lot about it," I say, impressed.

"I'm gonna join the league soon," says Jade. "I hope."

I watch the players race around the track, trying to pass one another and avoid flying elbows and shoulders that their competitors throw to block them.

"I can see why they need pads," I say.

"Go, Box-Out Betty!" shouts Jade at the top of her lungs, standing up and raising a fist in the air.

She sits back down and stares at the track. "Aren't those girls just beautifully badass?" she says wistfully.

"They really are," I say, wondering if I could ever take the knocking and bruising with such ease. I'm kind of a wimp. When I see one of the women get a bloody nose all over her rhinestone halter, I have to look away.

"Wanna get a snack?" I ask.

"Sure," Jade says, walking with me to the concession stand, but not taking her eyes off the rink.

"So how do you feel about seeing Rick on Monday?" I ask when we get out of the loud section of the stadium.

"Okay," she says. "I mean, better than I did Friday night when I had that crying jag."

I give her a sympathetic look.

"Ugh, sorry about that," she continues. "I acted like such a tool."

"Nah," I say. "It's totally understandable. Rick's the one who should be embarrassed, taking advantage of you like that."

"Hey!" says Jade, swatting my arm. "I did the seducing, you know."

"True," I say. "You're such a vamp."

She laughs and orders a ginger ale. I'm glad she's feeling better, but I'm sure there's more drama to come on Monday. You can't hook up with your boss and have things at the office be normal.

When we get back to our rinkside seats, Jade tells me to be quiet.

"Huh?" I ask.

"You're getting that song stuck in my head," she says. "If that happens, I won't be able to stop singing it for hours."

"What song?" I ask.

"The one you've been humming, like, all day," she says.

What is she talking about? "What are you talking about?" I ask.

"Quinn, there is hard rock pumping through these speakers, and you're obsessing over some old country song," she says. "I think it's by Loretta Lynn, right? My dad used to love her."

I tune into my subconscious and hear a B-side track on Russ's mix running through my head. "It's from the mix," I say, almost to myself.

"What mix?" asks Jade absentmindedly. She's watching someone from the Texecutioners get taken down hard. The derby girl slams into the ground after an elbow gets thrown at her from the side.

"Oh, nothing," I say. "Just this thing Russ made."

"Russ?!" Jade asks, snapping her head toward me. "He made you a mix?"

"It's not really like a *mix* mix," I say. "It's

more like his way of trying to get me to like country music."

"He probably wants to get you to like more than country music," says Jade. "He wants you to like country *guys*. And from the tone of your humming, it sounds like it's working."

"Is not!" I shout.

"Whatever," says Jade.

I focus on the game in front of me, where one skater named Daisy Hazzard is passing everyone and earning huge cheers from the crowd.

"He's getting to you, isn't he?" asks Jade. "This frat cowboy."

"No," I say. "I'm really into Sebastian."

Jade perks up then.

"He's so completely hot," she says. "So are you guys full-on dating or what?"

"I think so," I say. "I mean, we've been hanging out, like, twice a week."

"Right," says Jade. "Definitely. He's yours. Unless you're starting to like someone else or something. . . ."

"I'm not," I say.

"Okay, cool," says Jade, sipping on her straw and getting back into the game.

"Go, Chrisifier!" she stands up and shouts as a buxom blond girl with awesomely ripped thigh muscles makes another successful loop around the track.

When Chrisifier faces me, I freeze. *It's Chrissy!*

"Oh my God, I know that girl," I say to Jade.

"Who, Chrisifier?" asks Jade. "She is balls-out competitive. I've seen her make other girls cry before—and this isn't a crying group of girls."

"Seriously?" I ask. "She's my cousin's sorority sister and she comes over all the time to watch romantic comedies—and *she* cries."

"That's so cool," says Jade, missing the part about Chrissy's penchant for cheesy movies. "You get to hang out with Chrisifier!"

"I had no idea," I say, as I watch her body-check another victim. *Do I really have Chrissy all wrong?* I hate to admit it, but I had her pegged as a girly girl who wears pink and weeps during *The Bachelor* and shrieks so loudly that my ears hurt when something scares her. That might all be true, but there's a lot more to this girl than

I assumed. Which makes me wonder who else I've maybe unfairly stereotyped.

I'm quiet for the rest of the game, and I don't let Chrissy see me before we leave.

"You don't wanna go say hi and congratulate her?" asks Jade. Chrissy's massive scoring power—not to mention her herculean defensive moves—definitely won the game for her team.

"Nah," I say. "I'll see her later."

On the drive back to the condo, I text Sebastian.

"Who are you texting?" asks Jade.

"My best friend from home," I lie. I don't want her to know that I'm actually asking Sebastian if he'll make me a mix of his favorite songs to spin right now. When I get that, I'll have proof that he and I have something going. And I'll have something else to listen to besides Russ's manipulative soundtrack.

"So what did you do yesterday?" asks Jade.

"I just hung out with my cousin," I say. "We listened to music mostly."

"Like Mr. Muscle's Mix?" asks Jade, laughing.

I don't respond.

When Jade drops me off, I walk up to the condo and unlock the door. Then I flop down on the couch, slip in my earbuds, and press PLAY. Music usually clarifies everything for me—helps me know how I feel, what I think, what the truth is. But right now the playlist I want to hear just confuses me more.

Chapter 14

When I get into work on Monday, Jade is wearing a summer jumpsuit in bright purple and her hair is definitely *done*. As in, red movie-star waves cascading down her tanned, exposed shoulders.

I look down at my Pursued by Bear concert T-shirt and, for the first time, feel a little . . . I don't know . . . frumpy?

"Someone's dressed to impress," I say, settling into my mail-opening corner.

"What ever do you mean?" asks Jade, batting her eyelashes at me.

We both start laughing.

"Not that it did me any good," Jade says. "Rick's out of town this week."

"That's convenient," I say.

"Yeah," she says. "Cowardly bastard."

I take in her smile and her straight-backed posture. Jade looks okay. She looks . . . over it.

"Hey, Quinn," she says, looking at me earnestly. "Thanks for this weekend."

"No big deal," I say.

"No, truly," she says. "I really appreciate you listening to me on Friday night. And the derby was so much fun—it was just what I needed."

"Sure," I say, using a box cutter to open the biggest box in the mail pile. It's a bunch of Chipped Nail Polish T-shirts—they're a new punk girl-band.

"Those are for a fall festival," says Jade. "Let's put them in the closet."

We walk to the back room and lift the heavy box onto a mid-level shelf. Being in here, I can't help but picture Jade hooking up with Rick. And then my own fantasy comes to mind. I imagine myself in here, making out with—

"So did you see Russ last night?" asks Jade.

I can't tell if she's mocking me or not. I also don't think she'd approve of Russ. I mean, he's not really her type, if Rick and Sebastian are any indication.

"Nope," I say. "He wasn't around. But

Sebastian's making me a mix of all his favorite songs from this summer."

I might be lying about that last part—I haven't heard back from Sebastian—but I'm sure he'll do that for me. I mean, 1) He's a DJ, and 2) We're pretty much dating. So why wouldn't he?

"That's romantic," says Jade. "Does he know he has competition in the mix department this summer?"

"No," I say. "He just wanted to make it." I feel bad lying to Jade, but sometimes I present situations in the way I *wish* they were. Like, I *wish* Sebastian would think to make me a mix on his own . . . but he hasn't. So I have to help it along. But Jade doesn't need to know that detail.

"Well, it sounds sweet," says Jade. "And I bet there won't be a single country song on it."

"Who knows," I say. "Maybe Sebastian has broader taste than you think."

And I suddenly realize that I hope he does.

This week, I go into Amalgam for a few hours each day, partly to help Jade out while Rick's gone, but also—I admit to myself—to avoid any Russ run-ins. With all the driving I'm doing, I can sing almost every song on his mix, lyric for lyric.

On Thursday afternoon, when I skip out of the office after a morning of unpacking boxes and mailing out CDs, I come home to find Russ sitting on the couch watching baseball.

"Priscilla!" he shouts when I walk in the door.

My stomach flip-flops when I see his smile, but I will myself to be cool. Besides, it's annoying that he's just over here, like he's allowed to enter my world anytime he pleases.

I drop my keys on the entryway table and give him an unenthusiastic "Hi."

"No thank-you for the mix?" he asks.

"Thanks," I say, lingering in the doorway.

"That'll do," he says. "For now."

I roll my eyes and walk into the kitchen.

"Ready to get wet?" he calls after me.

And although Barton Springs on a hot day is amazing, I just can't go back there with him.

"Not really," I say, opening the fridge to look for a snack. "I have some things to do."

"Like what?" asks Russ, calling my bluff.

I panic a little because I have *nothing* that I

need to be doing. My eyes dart to the kitchen island, where there's a half-used shell-pink polish that Penny was painting her nails with last night. "I have to, um, meet Penny for a manicure," I say.

Russ guffaws. That is actually the word I think of when he laughs—*guffaw*. It's huge and loud and it comes from deep inside, like he truly thinks I just said the funniest thing in the world.

"Come on!" he says. "We're going tubing!"

I wonder briefly if he needs me to come with him to buy materials to build a robot, but I find out soon enough that he's talking about us going for a ride down the Guadalupe River, which is about half an hour outside of Austin.

I'm about to protest some more, but then the phone rings.

It's Penny, who informs me that a bunch of the Tri-Pi sisters are coming over for chips and dips and fruity drinks before they go out tonight, so can I please make sure the living room is straightened up?

"I'm in," I tell Russ immediately after I hang up with Penny.

The orange bikini I wore to Barton Springs is still hanging downstairs in the half bathroom, and I change into it while Russ runs next door to get "supplies."

I meet him outside at his truck, completely covered in sunscreen. I brought the bottle with me so I can reapply all day and make sure he does too. I'm wearing my dark aviator glasses and wishing I had a hat. Luckily, Russ has a selection in his truck.

"I don't really want to wear a jock cap," I say, looking at all the UT frat hats in the backseat.

"That's what you need in the river," says Russ. "Anything else will fly off your head. Besides, these you can dunk in the water and not worry about it."

Practicality wins, and I put on an orange UT cap that matches my bikini. I am fully aware of the fact that if I take off the band T-shirt that's covering me, I'll look like a damn cheerleader.

When we get to the river and unload at the parking lot, Russ reaches into the back of his truck and grabs a dirt-covered pair of sneakers for me. "Put these on," he says. "They're river shoes. You'll lose those flip-flops."

I have a lot to learn about tubing. Russ rents a black rubber tube for each of us, plus an extra cooler-tube, which he fills with sodas and snacks from the store attached to the rental place. I help him carry our third-wheel tube out to the river, and then he ties it to his own tube with a cord.

"Seriously?" I ask.

"Seriously," he says. "This is how we roll down the Guadalupe."

I keep my T-shirt over Penny's bikini, which I still don't feel comfortable in. As soon as I push off the ground and start floating, I realize I forgot my sunscreen.

"Crap!" I shout. "I'm going to *burn*."

"Hey, 'Cilla," says Russ, raising his sunglasses to look me in the eye. "Relax, breathe, and try to have fun. You're too uptight sometimes."

He guffaws at me—*again*—and sits back in his tube.

Am I uptight? I don't think I'm uptight. I think *Russ* thinks I'm uptight, but he doesn't know me at all. He just met me and already he thinks he's so smart about what I should think and say and be. He doesn't even know—

Whoosh! I drop down a sloping rapid and almost flip over in my tube. I manage to hold on to the sides and get myself upright before I go entirely underwater, but the baseball cap that I borrowed from Russ is totally dunked. When I shake my head out and clear my vision, I see that he's right behind me, laughing.

And I start to laugh too. We're outside, floating down a river on a hot, sunny day and I'm sitting here worrying about my skin (which is already covered in SPF 80 from before I left the condo), my footgear, my whole *outfit*, for goodness' sake! Russ is right. I need to just *let go* and enjoy myself.

We're at a slow stretch of water, so Russ pulls the cooler to him as I paddle over to grab a Coke. Russ holds our tubes together with one hand and his soda with the other. He shares a bag of Doritos with me as we float.

"So, do you come here often?" I ask.

"Sometimes," he says. "I used to tube here when I was younger, with my dad. He loved to float down the river."

"That's cute," I say. I look over and see a little boy on the edge of the water aiming a water gun at his mom, who's sitting at a picnic table in their yard. She screams as he douses her.

"Were you like that kid?" I ask.

"So much worse," says Russ. "I used to set water balloons above the front door . . . *inside* the house."

"And have you matured since then?" I ask.

He grins and wipes a Dorito-cheesed hand on my arm.

"Gross!" I shout, leaning over to wash off the orange powder.

He laughs and takes a sip of Coke.

We float quietly down the river like that for a while, and it's nice. I sort of enjoy Russ's company when he's not talking.

Soon we go over a small patch of rapids, which is really just a quick drop to a lower section of the river, and Russ lets go of my tube and I drift ahead.

"Are you over hanging on to me?" I joke.

"You're getting that song stuck in my head," he says. "If that happens, I won't be able to stop singing it for hours."

"What song?" I ask.

"The one you've been humming all day," he says. "'Waltz Across Texas.' It's the final track on the CD I made you, or at the end of Side B, if it's the tape you've been obsessing over."

He smiles at me with a triumphant twinkle in his eye.

"I don't know what you're talking about," I say, paddling my tube ahead of him so I won't have to acknowledge that his songs are getting into my head.

"Nothing to be ashamed of," says Russ. "That's my favorite song of all time. I'm glad you like it."

"I don't like it," I say stubbornly.

"Admit it!" Russ calls out. "You love my mix!"

I can hear him paddling from behind me and gaining speed.

"I do not!" I shout, smacking my hand through the water to splash him as he pulls up alongside me.

"Methinks she doth protest too much," says Russ.

I pout, looking off into the distance and pretending to focus on the next bend in the river.

"I'm really getting to you, aren't I?" asks Russ. "You're starting to have a crush on me."

"No," I say. "You're just around a lot. If someone's constantly there, it's like, you just think about them because they're around."

"Okay, Cleopatra, Queen of Denial," says Russ, lying back on his tube.

"I'm really into Sebastian," I say, looking over at Russ to gauge his reaction.

His sunglasses cover his eyes, but I see the muscles around his mouth twitch a little.

"I'm happy for you," he says, swinging the cooler around with his leg and opening it up for another soda.

I'm a little preoccupied for the rest of our float down the Guadalupe, but I try to push the awkward feelings aside and enjoy the cool water. I hum a hard-core London Rose song audibly, so Russ knows his mix is out of my head.

Luckily, it's going out of rotation soon. Sebastian texted me on Wednesday and asked me to come to Dirty's Friday night. And he said he has a present for me.

Russ and I don't talk much as we get to the end of our float and return the tubes. The drive home is quiet too, but it's not a bad kind of silence. We listen to a Loretta Lynn CD that he has—and Jack White is singing on it, too, which is pretty cool.

* * *

The next day, Jade and I are planning on going out to dinner when we leave Amalgam, and then heading over to Dirty's to see Sebastian deejay.

"Let's stop by your house first," says Jade.

"Why?" I ask.

"You'll see," she says.

Those two little words are ominous, but I dutifully pull in to the condo parking lot anyway.

When we walk in, Penny and Chrissy are racing around, cleaning. Penny has a bottle of Windex in one hand, and she's spraying it on every possible surface. She's also holding a wad of paper towels. Chrissy is vacuuming the rug under the couch, and all the chairs and tables have been moved to the walls.

"What's going on?" I ask.

"Ooh, Quinny! We're having a party!" says Penny.

Chrissy squeals in delight. "Everyone's been gone for a while, but now that it's getting closer to August, people are coming back. The semester starts in a month, and we're throwing the first big bash of the season."

"It's, like, tradition," says Penny.

I look over at Jade. "Did you know about this?" I ask. "Is this why you wanted to stop here?"

"No," she says. I see her staring at Chrissy.

"Oh, Chrissy and Penny, this is Jade," I say. "She's a big roller derby fan." I look at Chrissy pointedly.

"We saw you play last weekend," says Jade as Chrissy runs over to barrel her down with her signature-squeeze greeting.

Jade smiles as she hugs Chrissy right back. "You were awesome."

"Quinn!" shouts Chrissy as she pulls away from Jade. "You didn't tell me you were at my match!"

She looks over at Penny, who shrugs. "I didn't know Quinn liked all that bruiser stuff," she says.

I'm semi-relieved. I have feared that my cousin was going to reveal that her nickname was Penny the Punisher and I was going to have to reevaluate my impressions of all the Tri-Pis. But so far, only Chrissy has truly surprised me.

Jade still looks starstruck.

"The way you nailed Tess the Terminator

was incredible," she says.

"I broke a nail on that one," Chrissy whines. She holds up her Tri-Pi purple manicure.

"*Anyway,*" I say, looking at Jade. "What are we doing here?"

"I actually planned to get your cousin to help me pick out some hot clothes for you and do your hair for tonight."

"What?" I ask.

"Sorry, Quinn," Jade says. "But you are screaming for a makeover."

Penny drops the cleaning spray and paper towels so she can clap her hands together with glee.

"Party makeover!" she screams. Chrissy joins in.

I glare at Jade, feeling betrayed by someone who I thought understood me and my dislike of superficial fashion-and-beauty crap.

"Look," she says. "If you want to seal the deal with Sebastian, and *really* make him your summer fling, you've got to work it a little bit harder."

I think back to her purple jumpsuit from Monday, and actually, all of Jade's looks. She's not pink-glossed and fake-lashed like Penny is when she goes out, but she's certainly got a style that I suppose *is* a notch up from my band tees and jeans.

I look around the room at their faces. Jade has one eyebrow raised, probably worrying that she's offending me. Penny and Chrissy share identical looks of hope, wide-eyed and ready to grab the curling iron.

I stare down at my Converse.

"Okay," I say. "But no high heels."

Upstairs in the bathroom, I am subjected to all kinds of torture. First, they make me strip down to my bra and underwear.

"We start from the bottom up," says Penny as if this "party makeover" is a reality show that she's hosting.

They turn on the crazy light globes that frame Penny's bathroom, and Chrissy pulls out a magnifying mirror that retracts from the wall — something I'd never noticed. "It's for really looking at your pores," she says. "And plucking."

Penny's perfectly groomed eyebrows are inches from my face as she pulls stray hairs from my natural arches.

"Please," I say. "Not Marlene Dietrich pencil brows."

Jade laughs and I catch her eye in the mirror. She mouths a *sorry* and I have to forgive her. She couldn't have known the excitement that a makeover would cause in this condo.

After a sudsy scrubbing that leaves my face a little raw, Chrissy gets out cotton balls and tones my cheeks while Penny waits in the wings with moisturizing cream. Then they start in on the makeup.

"Here's where I take over," says Jade, tapping Penny on the shoulder.

My cousin looks momentarily crushed as she hands over the foundation puff, but I'm so glad I won't be made up to look like a Tri-Pi pledge. Jade grabs eyeliner and a dark lip stain, which she uses on my cheeks.

"Uh, that's for her lips," says Penny.

"Oh," says Jade, shrugging innocently. "Well, *it* doesn't know it's for her lips. It looks good on her cheeks—Quinn isn't really a Princess Pink girl."

I look up at Chrissy, but she's just nodding

at Jade's work. A few minutes later, after some close encounters with the mascara brush and one lipstick do-over (I turned my head at just the wrong moment), Jade steps back.

"You look super pretty, Quinn," says Penny, smiling in approval.

"Totally," says Chrissy.

But they won't let me turn around to see until they do my hair. Over the past few weeks, it has faded to a cool-but-weird aqua-blond color, and it's growing out, so it's a little messy. They mussed it with a bunch of mousse earlier, and Jade blew it dry while Penny and Chrissy were working on my eyebrows and skin care. I have no idea what it looks like right now.

"Pin it back with clips?" asks Penny, grabbing her basket of hair accessories, which is overflowing with purple Tri-Pi bows.

Jade shakes her head no. Since the makeup wonder she's worked, Penny and Chrissy seem to be deferring to her expertise.

"Headband?" asks Penny.

"Close," says Jade.

Then she tugs a thin, stretchy band out of her back pocket. It's a double-elastic and it's black. So it's like an accessory, but it's simple and not girly.

She pulls it over my head and pushes it back, pulling out a few strands in the front.

"Nice touch," says Penny. I don't think I've ever seen her give so much style credit to someone who's not a Tri-Pi.

"Gorge," agrees Chrissy.

Then they let me turn around and face the Hollywood-lit mirror.

My eyelids are lined in black liquid liner. It's pretty thick, but not in a creepy-looking way. And the soft auburn eye shadow almost makes my brown eyes look golden. My lips are a soft red, which I wasn't sure I could pull off, ever, but somehow I do. My hair is unbelievable. It's the perfect mix of done and undone—loose and a little bit wild around the edges, but tucked back with the black double-band, which contrasts with my pale hair really well.

I look like me, but hot.

"The Alpha-Alpha guys are going to die when they see you," says Chrissy.

"I cannot wait for this party," Penny chimes in.

I look up at Jade anxiously.

"We're actually going to Dirty's tonight," she says. "Sebastian is deejaying."

"Oh," says Penny, looking deflated. But she brightens up again in about half a second. "Wait! Who's *Sebastian*?"

"Quinn's boyfriend," Jade says at the same time that I say, "Just a guy."

Penny's eyes widen excitedly. "Bring him over after!"

"I think we're probably gonna go somewhere else," I say, knowing that it would *not* be cool to bring Sebastian to a Greek party. He would hate it.

"We can come back here," says Jade. "Come on, Quinn. . . . It'll be fun. Sebastian will love your cousin."

"Uhh . . . maybe," I say, seeing no way out.

"Closet time!" shouts Chrissy.

In Penny's room, Chrissy lays out a bunch of clothes in pastels with scalloped edges, and I have to draw the line.

"We did the bathroom part," I say. "Do we really need to go fully *Makeover Story* on me right now?"

Chrissy and Penny nod simultaneously: *Yes,*

we do need to do that. But Jade is more reasonable.

"Girls, she's not ready," says Jade. "But let's at least find your smallest band tee."

When we get to Dirty's, the bar is packed.

"Flannel Fades is playing later," says Jade. "They're *huge* here."

"Looks like some of the students are back too," I say, seeing way more burnt-orange hats in the crowd than usual.

We find space to lean against a wall near the DJ booth and I wave at Sebastian. He smiles and holds up a CD, handing it over the edge of the booth. It's the mix I asked for. I tuck it into my tattered canvas bag for later, and I resolve to replace Russ's mix with this one, at least outside of the car.

"I am so not bringing Sebastian back to Penny's," I say to Jade.

And then I think I see her roll her eyes ever so slightly.

"What?" I ask. "You think I *should*?"

"I think you should ask Sebastian if he wants to go back to your cousin's house," she says. "Tell him it's kind of a frat party, but that it could be fun, even if it's not his usual scene."

That actually sounds . . . wise. But still scary. Who can face that purple Tri-Pi decor without a little bit of a vurp?

"You really think he'll be cool with it?" I ask.

"I really think you should let him decide," she says. "At least give him a chance to meet these other people in your life."

"But they're not, like, my *friends*," I say.

Jade looks at me skeptically. "Yes," she says, "they are. And they're cool in their own way."

Then she turns around and her back is to me. I let her words sink in. It's not that I don't like Penny and Chrissy and their friends. Well, maybe I didn't like them at first. But I do hang out with them a lot at the condo, because they're there and I'm there and . . . I guess they kind of *are* my friends. They're just . . . not who I thought my friends would be.

When Sebastian finishes spinning, he joins us against the wall. We stay for Flannel Fades and I don't mention Penny's party until they finish their encore. Then Jade does it for me.

"There's a party at Quinn's cousin's condo tonight," she says.

Sebastian looks up at me with interest.

"It's a Tri-Pi and Alpha-Alpha party," I say quietly.

"Wait," he says, his grin widening. "A *what*?"

"Quinn's cousin is in a sorority," says Jade. "She's all insecure about it, but it'll be fun."

Sebastian shrugs like he doesn't really care. "Let's go," he says.

We pile into the Festiva and I pop Russ's tape out of the deck before I start the car.

"Put on the mix I made you," says Sebastian.

Jade knocks me on the shoulder in approval and I smile at her in the rearview mirror.

"I can't," I say, pointing to the tape player.

He laughs. "Whoa," he says. "I guess you should have specified that you wanted a taped mix."

Then he grabs Russ's cassette.

"'Indie plus country equals harmony,'" he reads. "Nice. I guess someone knew you had a tape player. Who made this?"

"Quinn's neighbor," says Jade.

"Yup," I say, starting the car.

"So mine wasn't your first Austin mix?" he asks.

"Second," I say, concentrating on pulling out of the parking lot.

"Well, that was nice of her to make this for you," he says.

Neither Jade nor I correct his pronoun.

Chapter 15

I can hear the party before we pull in to the condo parking lot. Mainly, I can hear hoots and hollers. Like, real hoots and hollers, as in "Yeehaw!" and "Wooooo-hooooo!" It's like they're staging a production of the musical *Oklahoma!*, with a keg.

I'm nervous.

Sebastian gets out of the car and pulls his seat-back up so Jade can exit too.

We walk into the party, and I'm imagining that record-scratch moment, where the music stops and everyone stares because they know we're not part of the Greek system, and maybe someone tries to beat up Sebastian because he's pale and kinda skinny. And then Jade gets in a "bitch!"-calling fight because she's tough and these sorority types like to make verbal digs at girls who don't look like they do.

But none of that happens.

When we open the door, Penny runs over to hug me and Jade, and then she introduces herself to Sebastian. He seems slightly over-whelmed by her glossy hair and blazing white teeth, but he still handles himself.

I relax a little bit and move into the party, saying hi to Chrissy and grabbing a cup from the kitchen.

"'Cilla!" I hear.

I turn and see Russ working the keg, smil-ing right over the crowd of people swarming around him and looking straight at me. He's waving the tap hose.

"You know the keg guy?" asks Sebastian. "That's a good thing, even if he did get your name wrong."

We go over together and Russ reaches out for my hand through the line of beer-seekers. Sebastian grabs on to my shirt and follows.

"You look beautiful," says Russ.

And it's this simple sentence that you think will mean nothing, because maybe your mom has said it to you a thousand times, or your best friend says it when you're having an inse-cure moment about your outfit. But it's not like that—it's completely different when a guy says it. I didn't know that until this moment, because it's the first time a guy has ever said it to me. Three words just gave me goose bumps, and I feel like a girly girl for a second.

"Your eyes . . . what's different?" asks Russ.

"Oh, I don't know," I say, tugging at the back of my hair self-consciously. "My friend Jade just helped me do my makeup."

"She did a good job," Russ says, grinning so his dimples deepen.

Sebastian noses up to the keg alongside me, pushing a little.

"Hey, how about you pour the beer, man?" he says to Russ, impatiently.

"What's up, DJ?" asks Russ, his lips tight-ening as he takes my cup first and fills it.

"My name's Sebastian," says Sebastian.

"Of course it is," says Russ, narrowing his eyes and pouring a lot of foam into Sebastian's cup.

Maybe this *is* going to turn into the scene I

imagined when we walked in.

But Sebastian doesn't seem to notice Russ's intensity. He just raises his cup in thanks before we walk out to the deck together.

It's hot outside, but not unbearable. Tonight is kind of nice, actually. I lean back on the deck railing and look up at the sky, which seems so huge here, like the earth opens up wider over Texas.

"So these are the people you hang out with?" asks Sebastian.

"Huh?" I ask, breaking away from my stargazing.

Penny comes outside and I can see her sizing up Sebastian behind his back. She gives me the thumbs-up, which means she thinks he's cute even though he's probably not her type. I appreciate that.

"So, Sebastian," she says. "Are you from Austin?"

He turns around to face her and smirks a little. "I'm originally from San Antonio," he says. "I came for the music."

"Cool," says Penny. "I love the Austin music scene too. And that's what got Quinn down here, after all."

The music changes and Rihanna is replaced by one of the songs on the mix Russ made me—it's actually a Wholaheys' song that's been rerecorded by a country artist, and it's not half bad.

Sebastian turns his back on my cousin.

"So you wanna finish these and get out of here?" he asks me.

"Uh . . ." I stutter, watching Penny's face fall for a second before she heads over to talk to a group of guys on the other side of the deck. She was just trying to be social, but Sebastian was pretty rude.

"The beers," says Sebastian, pointing to his cup like I'm being too slow for him. "We should finish them and then go somewhere else. I mean, frat parties *suuuck*."

"Yeah," I say, automatically affirming what I've always thought I believed. But the second after I say it, I realize I don't want to leave.

I stare through the glass doors and see Jade talking to Chrissy and two other Tri-Pi girls, throwing her head back and laughing at something someone's saying.

Then I look back at Sebastian, who is so obviously uncomfortable and anxious to go.

And in that moment I hear Russ's big booming laugh through the walls of the condo. I gaze in the kitchen window and I see him, smile blazing, bumping fists with everyone at the keg and laughing like the life of the party.

"I want to stay," I say to Sebastian.

"Come on, Quinn," he says. And his voice sounds whinier than I remember it being. "This isn't your scene."

I look at him evenly. "I live here," I say. "And these people are my friends."

"*That* guy is your friend?" Sebastian points to a frat brother of Russ's who's wearing one of those beer hats with the straw that leads straight to his mouth. His T-shirt says, C'S GET DEGREES.

"Okay, maybe not him specifically," I say. "But yeah, some of these people have kind of been here for me this summer." I glance over at Russ, just for a second.

Sebastian sighs in frustration. "Look, I know that Penny ditz is your cousin but—"

I feel my mouth draw closed into an angry line. "Did you just call my cousin a ditz?" I ask.

"Don't get all protective, Quinn," he says. "You told me that you think she's a complete airhead princess."

"I never said that!" I say.

"You did," says Sebastian.

"Well, I didn't mean it," I say, flustered. Have I really been going around talking about Penny that way? I feel a rush of guilt. And besides—she's my family, so I can talk about her. But he can't.

"You're not the same girl I met earlier this summer," says Sebastian. And the weird thing is, I think he's trying to hurt me by saying that I've changed. He's probably insinuating that I'm not as cool as I once was, that I've lost some sort of imaginary edge. But I don't care what he thinks, I realize. Sure, Sebastian's hot and he knows a lot about indie music and he makes for a good photo on my Facebook page. He looks like the kind of guy a girl like me would hang out with, go to shows with, be seen with.

But somehow, we don't fit.

"You should probably go," I say. "Since it's not really your scene."

He stares at me for a long moment before turning around, walking back through the sliding glass doors, and disappearing.

Not five seconds later, Penny's at my side.

"What was that about?" she asks, swirling the ice in her drink around with a tiny straw.

"He was being a jerk," I say.

"I'm glad you noticed," she says. "I thought you might be completely blinded by his metrosexual haircut."

I laugh. "Touché," I say. Then I pause and think about how to say what I want to say next.

"He really is a good guy," I say. "I think he was just uncomfortable here."

"Hmph," says Penny.

"Well, he's my type," I say, trying to defend Sebastian a little. "I mean, I like it when people are like me. And when they understand the music that I like, it feels like they understand a big part of who I am."

"Who you are or who you want the world to *think* you are?" asks Penny.

"What's that supposed to mean?" I ask.

"You've got your rock-short haircut, your indie internship, your DJ boyfriend," she says. "Does it all feel right?"

"Yeah," I say slowly. "It does." But as I hear myself talking, I realize that music taste is a flimsy reason to date someone.

"Are you so smitten with the DJ that you haven't noticed anyone else?" asks Penny.

"Who?" I ask.

"A certain lonesome cowboy next door," says Penny, possibly creating a new clichéd personal descriptor as she takes a sip from her drink.

"Russ?" I ask. "He's not into me. He just wants to prove that I'm wrong about things. He's like a stubborn ten-year-old."

Penny laughs and an ice cube flies out of her mouth. "He described you practically the same way," she says, wiping her face. "Right before he told me he was completely falling for you."

"He did not say that," I gasp.

"Well, not in so many words, but . . ." Penny starts. "I haven't seen him this gone for someone since—"

"Penny!" shouts Chrissy from across the room. "You've got to hear Jade's story about her boss. Get in here!"

Penny turns to me. "Coming?" she asks.

"I've heard that one already," I say. "I'll be in in a minute."

She leaves me outside on the deck, where I

catch my breath. I tilt my head to the sky and take in the stars, making a wish on one particularly sparkly one before I go inside to work up the nerve to pull Russ away from the keg.

I find Jade, Penny, and Chrissy talking to two other girls by the kitchen island.

"Quinn!" Jade shouts, looping an arm around my shoulder. "Meet my new friends Jessica and Ashley."

"Hi," I say to the two smiling girls across from me.

"These girls have amazing tips on how to spot a player," says Jade. "I am learning all the warning signs that Rick put out. I had no idea!"

"Rick sounds like a d-bag," says Penny.

"Total d-bag," echoes Chrissy. "I'd like to meet him in the roller rink."

"I might just find me an Alpha-Alpha boy tonight," Jade shouts, and a few interested heads turn our way.

The Tri-Pi girls laugh. I love that Jade is just fitting in and embracing this scene. I wonder why I haven't been able to do that. Even in my mind right now, I'm judging Ashley and Jessica for looking Barbie-ish and having Simpson sister names. I might be an asshole, I realize. Just like Sebastian.

I take a deep breath and look over at Russ. The beer line is thinning. I walk over to the sink and empty out my cup so I have an excuse to approach the keg.

"Hey," Russ says when I get close to him, smiling at me in this really endearing way that makes my heart loop around a little. "Where's Mr. DJ?"

"He left," I say.

"I'm sorry," says Russ, not looking sorry at all.

"I told him to go," I say.

"Did you now?" asks Russ, looking impressed.

"Yeah," I say, trying to sound nonchalant. "So, do you get a break?"

Russ lifts both fingers to his mouth for the double whistle. "Nate!" he shouts.

A hugely tall guy in an actual cowboy hat hurries across the room toward us.

"Take over for a few," says Russ, handing him the hose.

Nate nods, and Russ puts his hand on my back, leading me toward the front door. My heart is pounding, because it seems like Russ has been waiting for me to do this—to say something. To start something. And I wonder if I'll be able to.

But I shouldn't have worried.

The second we get outside, he pulls the door closed behind him and folds me in his arms. I feel his kiss before I can say anything. But this is exactly what I wanted to say, in a much more articulate way than I could have put it.

His chest presses against me as I reach up and put my hands in his curly hair. I'm gasping a little, but I can't come up for air. This makeout session rates about 1000 on the hot meter, and I don't want to stop.

Finally, Russ does it for me.

"Are you drunk?" he asks.

"No," I say honestly. My eyes feel heavy and hooded. I want him to keep kissing me.

"Did you lose a bet?" he asks.

"No." I laugh, looking up and into his eyes. "I like you."

"I like you too," says Russ, leaning in for more kisses. I meet him halfway to save time.

Then I hear a voice.

"Hey, Russ," says a soft twang.

His head jerks up. When he sees her, I notice, he instantly lets go of me. I feel my body temperature drop rapidly.

"Katie," he whispers.

"Yup," she says. "That's my name."

She sticks out her hand at me, like I'm supposed to shake it. But unless she's Russ's sister, I don't think I want to touch this girl.

"This is Quinn," says Russ. And I'm disappointed that he didn't call me Priscilla.

"Well . . . hi," says Katie, dropping her hand since I've made no move to take it. "Listen, Russ, can we go somewhere and talk for a few minutes?"

I look over at him, watching him react to her question, the same question I asked him about half an hour ago by the keg.

He lowers his eyes and looks at the ground when he says, "Sure."

Then he opens up the front door to Penny's condo, for me. "See you later, Quinn," he says.

And I don't know why I don't fight, why I don't demand to know who this "Katie" is, why

I don't make them both explain what the heck just happened to interrupt my best-kiss-ever. But I don't. I just walk inside in a daze. *Did I just put my heart in the middle of a highway and watch it get splattered by an eighteen-wheeler?* Because that's what it feels like.

I walk past the party revelry, up the stairs to Miss Tiara's room. She raises her head when I open the door, and licks my hand when I sit down next to her on the floor. I stare at the blank walls for a moment before I hear more footsteps on the stairs.

"Quinn?" Penny knocks on the door as she calls my name.

She pokes her head in and Jade is right behind her. They look at me worriedly as they join me on the floor. It's like we're in a séance circle around Miss Tiara.

"What happened?" asks Jade. "Did you have a fight with Sebastian?"

My night has been so crazy that I'm not sure where to start.

"Sebastian left," says Penny. "And Quinn was outside making out with Russ. Until Katie came back."

Wow. I guess my cousin is like the Ernest Hemingway of retelling other people's drama, because she knows where to start and finish, summing up my evening in three concise sentences.

I raise an eyebrow at her.

"I was spying on you through the window," she explains sheepishly. "I can't resist a romantic moment—even if it isn't mine."

"Wait," says Jade. "Slow down. When did Sebastian leave?"

"Maybe an hour ago," I say. "He kept asking if I wanted to get out of here and saying that it wasn't his scene and all that. I guess I just got tired of it. I mean, it's not like *you're* a Tri-Pi type, but you were having fun. And Russ said I was beautiful and I was looking at the stars and this song was playing and it just seemed like everything was—"

I pause and look at their faces. I'm rambling.

"Okay, fine," I say. "So we kissed and now he's out there with some Katie. Who the hell is Katie anyway?" I stare at my cousin, demanding an answer.

Penny sighs. "She's his ex," she says. "She was in London earlier this summer, doing some program with the history department, but she's back now."

"And she just happens to suddenly reappear in the middle of the best kissing ever?!" I ask.

"I don't think Russ knew she was coming back this weekend," says Penny. "Things ended pretty badly between them."

"How long were they together?" asks Jade.

"Almost two years," says Penny. "They met right at the end of freshman year."

We all look down at Miss Tiara's pillow. This is intense. I'm suddenly regretting a lot of things.

"I never should have told Sebastian to leave," I say.

"Quinn, it doesn't mean anything that this girl is back," says Jade. "So what?"

I look over at Penny, who's biting her lip.

"What?" I ask.

"Nothing," she says. "I'm not sure what it means that Katie's here now. I mean, I know Russ really likes you . . . but they were, like, in love."

I feel a sharp pain in my chest.

"You guys, I think I want to be alone," I

say. I have this urge to put on my headphones and curl up next to Miss Tiara. "Can I have a blanket and a pillow?" I ask Penny. "I'll sleep in here."

With the party raging downstairs, it's not like I really have a choice.

The next morning, I wake up to Miss Tiara licking my nose. I look at my iPod—it's 6:14 A.M. I stand up to avoid the Tongue and I walk into the bathroom to splash some water on my face. There are discarded cups all over the sink area, and they smell gross. My makeup, I see, has that morning-after stank to it. Usually I think that's a good look, but today it just reminds me that last night went in a weird direction that ended up with me feeling hurt. I sigh out loud and Miss Tiara growls softly in commiseration.

"Let's take a walk," I say to her, heading to her closet to find her Juicy tank top. The fact that I'm dressing up this dog for a walk is something I would never admit to Raina back home, but the truth is, she does seem to like it. I grab the leash and step outside.

It's really quiet this early in the morning,

and as we stroll along the sidewalk of the condo complex, I kind of appreciate not having my iPod on right now. I can hear my own thoughts. And my brain is buzzing.

I keep turning over in my mind how Russ isn't my type, how he's the most frustrating person I've ever met, how incompatible we are. Raina would die if she saw how *Texas* he is, with his grass-in-mouth, cowboy smile, big-buckle-wearing self. And Raina would also die in a different way if she saw Sebastian in person—he's so perfectly indie, and exactly what I wanted in a summer fling. So what if he felt uncomfortable last night? It's the kind of party where *I* would definitely feel weird if I didn't know any of my cousin's friends. Didn't Penny scare me when she first picked me up this summer?

But then I think about Jade, and how she can fit in anywhere, in the indie scene, here at sorority central, with Rick and the bands on Amalgam. In lots of ways—minus the hooking up with our boss part—Jade is the girl I want to be.

And Russ, even though he's such a truck-driving, baseball-cap-wearing frat guy I could never see myself with, he's always himself.

He doesn't change for people. He knows who he is.

All these thoughts are in my head floating around, sorting themselves as Miss Tiara and I meander through the complex. The main one, though, is the kissing. I can still feel the fireworks inside me when I let my mind linger on Russ's lips.

But then I see her face—Katie. I mean, I really see it. She's right in front of me as I lead Miss Tiara back up the steps to Penny's front door.

"Hi," she says. She's still wearing the generic black tank dress she was in last night, and the stupid ribbons on her wedge heels are untied, I notice. She's fishing around in her purse.

I watch, openmouthed, as she finds her car keys and opens the door to a white Lexus parked in front of Russ's condo. Then she drives away, and I swear to ban all thoughts of those kisses from my mind. Forever.

I go back inside and delete Russ's playlist from my iPod, making a mental note to smash his tape later.

And then I start to cry.

Chapter 16

$\mathcal{I}$ spend Saturday and Sunday moping around. I make Penny close all the blinds so that Russ can't look in and see what we're doing. Part of me thinks that he'll come over at some point to explain, but he doesn't. And I'm done crying. Hour by hour I get angrier.

I consider calling Sebastian, but I figure he's still mad.

I'm a mess of indecision, so I decide to do nothing. My dad used to tell me that sometimes the best way to handle a crisis is: "Don't just do something, stand there!" It's Zen or Buddhist or something. It seems like the smartest thing right now. I email Mom and Dad to update them about . . . well, nothing really. I just tell them I'm having fun and helping to plan a big music festival. It's enough to keep them at bay for a while, I know. When they're traveling on these research trips they get all lost in their own world anyway.

Penny ropes me into watching a full season of *Sex and the City* on DVD, and those women are way older but they still are just as confused about guys as I am. It doesn't make me feel better, but eating a pile of candy from Penny's emergency bowl (which includes mini chocolate bars and reams of those button candies) eases my heartache a little.

On Monday morning, Jade is anxious to get an update from me, but I'm not in the mood to talk.

"Put on Fans of Emptiness," I say, and she dutifully loads the stereo with the dark and sorrowful band's most emo album.

"That bad?" she asks.

"Let's just say I saw Katie leaving Russ's condo at around seven A.M. Saturday morning, wearing her dress from the night before," I say.

"Ouch," says Jade.

Then Rick walks through the door. In the midst of my drama, I forgot that he was back this week. I glance at Jade to see how she reacts.

"Hi, Rick," she says, smiling cheerfully.

"Jade, Quinn." He nods, handing me some of the mail from the P.O. box and then walking back to his office without meeting either of our eyes.

"What was that?" I whisper once he's out of earshot.

Jade rolls her eyes. "Who knows?" she says. "I'm just going to be a good little intern, at least at work."

"And outside of work?" I ask.

"That's where I get to act like a crazy scorned lover," she says, laughing. I'm not sure she's joking, but I laugh along with her.

"Penny thinks I should be strong and single this summer," I tell Jade.

"What do you think?" she asks.

"I think she knows I have no shot with Russ now, and she just isn't into Sebastian," I say.

"Well, the question is: Are you into Sebastian?" Jade asks. Then I see her glance at the door. "Speak of the devil," she whispers under her breath.

Sebastian's standing in the entrance. *Could this office be more crowded with angst?* He shifts his weight awkwardly from one foot to the other.

"Um, Quinn?" he asks. "Can I talk to you

outside for a sec? If, um, it's okay?"

"Sure," I say, handing Jade the box cutter I was using to open packages. I briefly consider taking the stubby knife outside with me, but I think that would look weird. I may be a little bit mad at him, but I don't want to carve him up. Besides, I'm the one who kissed someone else on Friday night, which maybe wasn't allowed.

I stand up and brush off my jeans, following him to the parking lot. We sit on the curb in front of the neighboring UPS store, out of Jade's sight range, which I know will drive her crazy.

"I'm sorry about Friday night," he says. "I was a little buzzed and I flashed back to some weird frat parties I'd been to. I just needed to get out of there. But it wasn't cool to diss your cousin or her friends."

"Thanks for saying that," I say, picking up a stick and poking it into the top lace hole of my sneakers.

"Yeah," he says. "I just sometimes get weird around jock types. High school memories and all. The kid with the turntables wasn't really cool in my Friday Night Lights small town."

"I get it," I say. And I do. After all, don't I have

the same kind of chip on my shoulder? "Besides, that guy with the beer hat might have been asking for it." I bump Sebastian's foot with mine.

"Yeah, but even that guy deserves a little understanding," he says, smiling at me.

I smile back.

"Are we cool?" he asks.

"Yes," I say. "We're cool."

Sebastian kisses me on the cheek and I stand up to go back inside. "I have to do some work," I say.

"Can I call you this week?" asks Sebastian.

"Yeah," I say. "I'd like that."

And Sebastian does call. He wants me to go out with him on Wednesday night, and it's not a day too soon.

Katie's obnoxious Lexus has been parked next to my yellow Festiva for two days now. I've just barely resisted the urge to key it. I know that would be tacky, but it's tempting. Jade even told me about some country song about keying an ex-boyfriend's car, and I admitted that country songs can be pretty hard-core sometimes.

"They were together for a long time," says

Penny, defending Russ and Katie for the thousandth time as I get ready for Sebastian to pick me up.

"Penny!" I shout. "I told you: I don't care. Russ is an asshole and it's not my concern who assholes date or what assholes do, even if the asshole lives next door."

"He's your friend," says Penny.

"Whose friend?" I ask. "Your friend!" I point my mascara wand at her.

I've done well over the past few days after I convinced Penny that we had to stop watching *Sex and the City* and we had to start listening to a little seventies punk. That helped. So did pulling all the magnetic ribbon out of Russ's mix tape and then smashing the cassette shell. Incredibly satisfying.

It's only late at night, when I'm trying to fall asleep, that I see a sad montage in my head. As much as I try to block it out, I go back to our first burger, the day buying the Festiva, the night the bats didn't fly, Russ's hair in the sunset. But if I turn the Clash up loudly enough, I can drown out those images. Because now Katie's back.

Chapter 17

I take a deep breath and focus on the fact that Sebastian is picking me up, and he is hot and nice and smart about music. I must have been temporarily insane to think Russ and I had a shot at being together this summer. The man wears a giant brass belt buckle!

"Quinn," whines Penny, making a pouty face. "I can't go through the rest of the summer with you fighting with Russ. He's one of my best friends. Even Chrissy is afraid to come over because she knows you're mad."

"Well, has he made *one freaking attempt* to apologize to me for kissing me and then ditching my ass on the front step?!" I shout, more loudly than I mean to.

I throw the mascara I'm holding on the counter and bound down the stairs, acknowledging internally that I might be more upset than I want to be about this. I slam the door and sit on the front stoop, not wanting to listen to my cousin anymore, but also knowing that it's not her fault. I shouldn't be taking this out on her.

I'm staring at the shiny white Lexus and having another keying fantasy, when I hear the screen door to Russ and Chrissy's condo creak open. I sigh and brace myself for an impish laugh or possibly the sight of Russ and Katie lip-locked in a mirror image of *our* kiss from Friday night.

When I turn my head, though, I see Katie looking at me. Her eyes are red and puffy, and her face is streaked with tears. I can tell because her foundation has pale rivulets running through it. I never really get people who wear foundation. She looks so sad, though, I almost feel sorry for her.

Then she opens her mouth, and I think she might apologize or something.

"Bitch," she says, walking down the steps and huffily getting into her car.

I retract that thought about feeling bad for

her, and I give her the finger as she drives away. I look back up at Russ's door, wondering if he's going to follow her, wondering what happened, what prompted the B-word.

Vroom, vroom. Sebastian's Vespa pulls up and he holds out a helmet for me. I walk down the steps to him and slip it over my impossible-to-mess-up hair, trying to wipe thoughts of Russ from my mind.

Sebastian surprises me by driving down to Town Lake, near the Four Seasons where I sat with Russ just a couple of weeks ago. He parks the Vespa and opens up the seat where he has a small blanket folded up inside.

"What's this?" I ask.

"You wanted to see the bats, right?" he asks. "Jade told me that you tried to go once but they didn't fly."

"Yeah," I say, not wanting to think about being here with Russ . . . and now with Sebastian. "But aren't we going to a show? I mean, we don't want to miss what might be an incredible opening band that no one knows about yet and we need to get a spot up front for Gloria Airlines and what if there's a crowd already there and—"

Sebastian stops my rambling with a well-timed kiss. "I thought you would want this," he says when we break apart. "It's my weak attempt at sunset romance."

"I appreciate it," I say. "But I'd rather just go to the shows."

Sebastian shrugs and folds up the blanket, putting it back under the seat.

"As you wish," he says.

And what I really wish is that I'd stop being so ridiculous and start appreciating the guy who's right in front of me. The guy who's trying to win me over and not pushing me aside. But for some reason, I can't.

Later that night, after Gloria Airlines and their opener, Crimson Sun, both perform dizzyingly great sets, Sebastian takes me back to the condo. I'm still humming the encore song, which was so full of emotion that, at the show, I leaned back on Sebastian and just swayed with him, like we're really together. He gets off the Vespa and we walk to the front door holding hands. He tries to kiss me as I look for my keys, and though

I want to, I really want to, I just can't do it *here*. But that doesn't mean I can't do it anywhere.

"Let's go inside," I say, pulling the front of his T-shirt as we walk into the living room and fall onto the couch together.

I laugh and he smoothes back my hair, kissing my forehead and then moving to my cheeks and my lips, all the while pressing down on me as we sink into the cushions. It feels good to be close to him like this, and I will my mind to stop comparing his kisses, his shoulders, his hair to anyone else's.

"Wait," I say, sitting up and searching for my iPod. I find it and plug it into the stereo, turning the volume up as loud as I think I can without waking Penny. With the Walters on in the background, I can drown out any thoughts of that country cowboy next door, and let myself go.

In the morning, I hear Penny coming down the stairs. I open my eyes a crack and feel my shoulder wedged into the back cushions of the couch. Sebastian's arm is flung across my waist, and our legs are tangled together. I recognize there's no way I'm going to escape this position before Penny—

"Morning, Quinn," she says in a singsong voice.

I grunt a hello but don't lift my head. Sebastian doesn't move.

I hear Penny grab something from the kitchen and then she's gone, probably to plan some lavish sorority event or devious Rush hazing. When she pulls the door shut, Sebastian opens one eye.

"Hi," he says sleepily.

I sit up and realize that, although my jeans are unbuttoned, they're still *on*. Same with Sebastian's. I stand and head into the kitchen, zipping up and planning on making some sort of fruit bowl for us. *Is this what you do following a boy sleepover, which is broken Parent Rule #3? You make someone breakfast?*

I haven't dealt with the morning-after etiquette, really, because, well, I lived with my mom and dad before this summer. Hookups usually ended while it was still dark. This feels weird.

"Um, do you want some fruit?" I call to Sebastian, who's yawning and stretching on the couch.

"Nah," he says. "I should get going." He grabs his keys from the coffee table and I walk him out.

When he steps through the door I lean in to give him a kiss. It feels boyfriend-girlfriendy, and I like it. Then I stand there in my over-size T-shirt and bare feet, watching him zoom away.

"Priscilla." I hear Russ's voice, gruffer than usual, and I turn to look in his direction. He's standing in front of his condo wearing a wrinkled T-shirt and cargo shorts. His eyes are bloodshot—he looks like he hasn't slept. "We need to talk," he says.

Chapter 18

I have the urge to march inside and slam the door, but I'm also curious. Russ hasn't spoken to me since Friday night, and Katie's tear-streaked foundation face made me wonder . . . did he break up with her?

Not that I care, because after last night I am definitely *with* with Sebastian.

"Okay," I say, deciding to go the completely apathetic route.

He steps down to the sidewalk and walks up to my door.

"Can we go inside?" he asks.

"Oh, is this going to be a long talk?" I ask, folding my arms across my chest.

"Please?" he asks.

And because I'm committed to my not-caring stance, I shrug and turn around, letting him walk into the condo behind me.

The couch is a tangle of pillows-and-blanket, which I'm glad he sees. I walk straight back to the kitchen and perch on one of the bar stools by the island. It feels less friendly than sharing a seat at the table or on the mussed couch.

"Listen," says Russ, leaning across the island and looking down while he talks. "I know you must be mad at me right now."

"Not really," I say. I grab an apple and take a bite out of it nonchalantly, like, *Who cares what you're saying because I'm enjoying this delicious apple for breakfast and my day is going to be lovely and you have no effect on it.*

"I can tell you are," says Russ, glancing up at my face.

I feel a flicker of a frown cross my lips, but I try hard to shift it into a smile.

"I'm okay," I say. Then I jump up and go to the fridge to pour myself some orange juice, just in case I can't control my facial muscles if he keeps talking.

"Well, you should be mad as hell," he says. "I know I would be."

I pause at the open refrigerator door for a

second, but then I regain my balance and take out the orange juice. I grab a glass from the cabinet and pour slowly, with my back to Russ.

"I'm fine," I say.

"If that's true, then I'm glad," says Russ. "Because I feel like shit."

"Is that because you broke up with your girlfriend?" I ask, and I can't help the flash in my eyes when I turn around to face him.

"We were already broken up," he says. "I just finalized it."

I stay silent. I want to ask him, *What the eff happened? We were kissing! I was melting into you!* But instead I crunch into my apple again.

"Katie was gone for a month," says Russ. "And before she left, she ended things. Four weeks ago, if you'd asked me what I'd give for a chance to get back with her, I would have said anything. I'd give anything."

This is really not what I want to be hearing. I stand up and walk over to the sink, slowly pouring out my orange juice. I can't eat an apple and have orange juice—mixing fruits is weird. It was just a prop, and now I'm getting rid of it. Because I'm about to ask Russ to leave anyway.

I'm not a late-night-radio love DJ who wants to listen to his romantic problems.

"But then I met you," he says.

I stare out the window over the sink. Beyond the deck, there's a squirrel climbing on Penny's bird feeder, making it swing wildly back and forth.

"And you thought I'd be a fun distraction while Katie was away," I say, still watching the to-and-fro of the bird feeder.

"You know that's not it," says Russ. "For a girl with such a high opinion of herself, you've got a real insecure side. I like you, Priscilla."

I whirl around to face him. "So that's why you walked away with Katie the second you heard her voice?" I ask.

He looks down at the island, staring at the candy jar like there's an adequate response in there, between the red Twizzlers and the purple Nerds packs.

A good ten seconds pass. If he's not going to argue with me anymore, it's going to be a lot easier to let him go.

But then he starts talking again.

"It wasn't like that," he says. "We had stuff

to discuss. When she left at the beginning of the summer, I was really angry. Things are okay now—they're more clear. Katie and I are over. For real."

"Is that why she was crying outside your door last night?" I ask.

"Are you trying to make this as painful as possible?" asks Russ.

"No," I say. "I don't think this needs to be painful at all. At least not for me, because I'm not involved. And I don't even know why you're telling me any of this—it's between you and Katie, whatever your relationship is."

Russ bangs his hand on the island, and I jump. "Damn, Priscilla," he says. "I'm telling you it's over with her. And if you'd shut up for a minute I'd be able to tell you it's because of you."

I stare at the candy jar now, my eyes riveted to the peppermint swirls and the miniature Krackle bars for a nanosecond, the time it takes for me to regain my footing and remember that *I don't care.*

"Spare me," I say. I'm not strong enough when I say it—even I can hear the noncommittal tone I'm using. I mean for it to end the conversation, to shut him up. But it doesn't.

"Priscilla," Russ says, his voice pleading. "You're different, and fun, and unlike any girl I've ever met. I thought I'd never laugh so hard as when we talked. You're smart as a whip and stubborn as a mule!"

And then he's smiling at me with those big dimples, blue eyes twinkling like he thinks he's got this one in the bag, that I'm about to run over and kiss him with relief and joy. *He has ditched the ex-girlfriend for good! He has chosen me!*

But the timing is wrong. This isn't our moment. Past where Russ sits I can see the rumpled blankets from Sebastian's night here.

"I appreciate it," I say. "It's nice that you were so . . . impressed by my whip-and-mule-like qualities."

Russ looks confused.

"And I'm glad it helped clear things up with Katie too," I continue. "I mean, closure is always good, right?"

I give him a friend smile, resisting the urge to pat him on the shoulder. That would be overkill.

He still doesn't say anything.

"Listen, Russ," I say. "I'm sorry that I kissed you last week. It was stupid. I'll take full responsibility for my complete lack of judgment."

"But didn't you want . . ." he starts. And for the first time, I see that he's unsure of what he's saying. He's almost stuttering. "I mean, didn't you feel something?"

I take another bite of apple to keep myself from blurting out *Yes, you moron! I felt EVERYTHING*. But what I really say is: "Sure. I felt a little tipsy." I say this with my mouth full, which allows me to control my expression as I lie. I'm a bad liar, but food props help. "I mean, it was just a kiss."

I walk over to the trash can and throw out the core, wiping my hands on my shirt after it's gone. When I turn back to him, I hear a sigh on his lips. He looks sadder than Katie did yesterday, even with those streaks all down her powdery face.

He stands up to leave, walking over to the sliding glass door, ready to exit through the back. He opens it halfway. I'm standing by the sink, concentrating on picking apple bits out of my fingernails, but I can feel him turn to face me.

"It was more than a kiss to me," says Russ. "Just so you know."

Then he leaves and closes the door behind him. I wait a couple minutes, frozen, examining my fingernails. When I'm sure he's gone, I walk into the living room and press PLAY on the iPod, letting it shuffle to any song it chooses. Then I flop down on the couch with my head buried in a pillow. I hate crying out loud.

Chapter 19

By the time Penny gets home, I'm banging around the kitchen. I've dried my tears from this morning—I will not let Russ ruin my summer! I'm making chocolate chip cookies, which is the only homemaker-y thing my mom ever did with me when I was little. There's something very calming about measuring oil, sifting flour, and dropping little spoon-sized plops of dough onto a baking sheet. It's a cathartic ritual, and I'm primed for some catharsis. Maybe I'll even bring some cookies to Sebastian later. I wonder if he would think that was weird.

"Ooh, chocolate chip!" says my cousin, clapping her hands together and perching on the island stool. "What brought out your inner Donna Reed?"

"Nothing," I say, watching Miss Tiara jump

into her lap. I have the dog dressed in an apron that matches the pink-checked one I'm wearing. It's Penny's, of course, and I almost can't believe I actually dressed up the dog, but I think we look cute together, in a make-me-wanna-puke and I'd-never-let-anyone-see-me-in-this kind of way.

"Okay, so good goss," says Penny, leaning across the island and pinching a bit of dough and chips between her fingers.

I slap her hand quickly as I await her "goss."

"Russ broke up with Katie," she says in a whisper, raising her eyebrows expectantly, and ignoring my slap.

"I know," I say, turning around to put batch number one in the oven.

"Well, aren't you happy?" she asks.

I set the baking timer for eleven minutes and face my cousin. "Why would I be?"

"Uh . . . because you guys kissed last week-end and then when you thought he was back together with Katie you practically melded to the couch in deep depression, which was only alleviated by my genius romance-crisis plan involving *Sex and the City*." Penny leans over for another swipe of cookie dough and I snag the bowl before she can get to it.

"That was before last night," I say. "Sebastian and I are together now for real."

Penny pouts and I put the bowl down again, within her reach.

"Besides," I continue. "I was just confused and lonely. Russ isn't my type."

"Ooh, if I hear you say that one more time, I'm going to scream!" says Penny. "You are completely blind, Quinn!"

After one last pinch of dough, she stomps off, up the stairs to her room. Miss Tiara abandons her sous-chef duties and follows Penny. Traitor.

I pick up my phone and text Sebastian, making sure we're on for Friday night at Dirty's. I'll bring him cookies and hopefully we can have another sleepover. That should prove to everyone that I'm with him, and that I'm not supposed to be with Russ.

Right?

The next two weeks go by in a blur. Things have picked up at Amalgam as Rick plans for the big summer festival in August. Jade has been on the phone arranging travel for a lot of the bands, so I'm handling all her normal intern duties, like sending out press kits and prioritizing demos for Rick to listen to. I'm going into the office almost every day. Between work and nights out with Sebastian (he liked the cookies), I haven't had a chance to breathe—let alone think about Russ. And that has been a good thing.

When I call Raina to check in for our first off-line catch-up in almost three weeks, she has news of her own. She's dating a new theater employee named Eddie.

"Isn't that kind of a dog's name?" I ask.

"More like a rock star name," she says.

"Okay, okay, so what's he like?" I ask. "Wait! Is this that big nerd you told me about earlier this summer? The one who's way into science fiction?"

"Yeah . . ." she starts. "But he's growing on me!"

"Really?" I ask skeptically.

"Yes!" says Raina, and I can hear her smiling. "He wears skater shorts and has lots of pins on his vest to make it individualized. And he's a film major, so he knows a ton about movies—his favorites are those Armageddon ones, like old stuff from the seventies that I've never really seen. He's planning a full marathon of influential sci-fi for us this weekend."

"Sounds fascinating," I say sarcastically.

"Shut up!" Raina laughs. "Okay, so he's a little nerdy, maybe not as ideal as Mr. Perfect Sebastian."

"Well, we can't all have the Supreme this summer," I say.

"I kind of think he *is* my Supreme," says Raina, and I can hear the giddiness in her voice. "At least, for right now. I'm serious, Quinn—I couldn't be happier with anyone."

"Really?" I ask. "You're falling hard for a sci-fi geek?"

"Yeah," she says. "I guess I am."

"Okay, so tell me what else you love," I say.

Raina answers without hesitation. "He holds the popper doors open for me when I'm scooping popcorn, and he always asks me how my day's going. He recommends books to me because he noticed I'm a big library girl. Oh, and he does this really cute thing where he'll wait for me to close at night, even though his shift sometimes ends a couple of hours earlier. He just sits in the lobby reading a paperback until I'm done."

I think about how, when Sebastian isn't spending the night, he doesn't even wait in the parking lot to see that I get in the door safely. He's slept over four times now, but he's never once stayed for breakfast. And he's rude to waiters.

"Quinn?" asks Raina. "Are you there?"

"Yeah," I say. "Sorry. Um, Penny's calling me, so I'd better go."

"Okay," she says. "I'll upload a picture of Eddie tonight, so check my profile later."

"Cool," I say. "Bye."

When I hang up, I don't want to feel jealous of my friend, but I do. How did she get *the* guy, while I ended up with someone who *looked* like the guy?

Chapter 20

On Friday afternoon, I'm spread out at the dining room table, organizing demos I took home from Amalgam. I've had one particularly angsty band, the Gas Station Horrors, playing on repeat as I ponder my mess of a love life.

Penny comes in carrying a bunch of poster board and a bag full of art supplies.

"It's time to make signs for Rush!" she says excitedly. Then she notices the drawn blinds and the somber tunes.

"Quinn," she says, "the brooding thing is getting old. Between you and Russ I can't deal. Can't we listen to something upbeat?"

"What do you mean?" I ask. "Is he upset about something?"

"I'm not getting in the middle of this," says Penny.

"Middle of what?" I ask, stopping the Gas Station Horrors in the middle of a dark song called "Pain at the Pump."

"Are you some sort of vampire?" asks Penny, ignoring my question.

I'm too emotionally exhausted to argue as she opens the blinds and lets in the way-bright sun. Then she starts laying art supplies out on the table, pushing my demos to the side.

"Dude!" I say. "I'm working here."

"Don't you want to help me make signs?" she asks. "If you don't, there will be hearts and stars all over these posters. Maybe you can create something that will draw in a different crowd this year?"

"Do you *want* a different crowd, Penny?" I ask a little snottily. "I thought Tri-Pi was all about tradition and sameness. As in, perky smiles, glossy hair, and possibly fake boobs."

She frowns at me.

"You really think that's all there is to me, don't you?" she asks.

"What?" I ask.

"I'm the sorority girl who is completely one-dimensional," she says.

"I was half kidding," I say.

"Yeah . . . *half*," says Penny, looking back down at her blank board. "You know, I think Russ was right about you."

"What do you mean?" I ask, defenses up immediately. *Can I spend one second not thinking about him?*

"He told me when you first got here that he thought you wouldn't hang out with us much because you'd be afraid of how it looked," she says.

"Why would he say that?" I ask.

"I guess he had a hunch after our first night at Shady Grove," she says. "You can be a little prickly sometimes, Quinn."

"Was that because I said I didn't like country music?" I ask. "Well, soooorry." But even as my instinct is to react like this—defensively—it doesn't feel right. Penny's not trying to insult me, she's trying to tell me something. And I recognize that she's not all wrong, that I do have my own preconceptions about sorority girls and boys in big buckles. Not to mention floppy-haired DJs.

Penny frowns. She starts to make glue swirls on her poster board, presumably for glitter to stick to later. I think back to the time I've spent with Chrissy, who completely surprised me with her roller derby action, and who is so genuinely herself in a way that most people aren't. I remember how excited Penny was when she first picked me up at the airport. Okay, her excitement scared me a little (as did her bright white teeth), but it was real. And then I think about how eager my cousin was to console me after Russ left me cold.

I'm acting like an ass.

"Penny," I say, "I'm sorry."

"You are?" she asks, pausing in midair with a glitter shaker in her hand.

"I am," I say.

"Why are you sorry?" she asks, being coy. She wants me to acknowledge some wrongs.

"Well . . ." I say, not really wanting to admit to specifics. "I guess I have kind of been assuming things about you."

Penny doesn't look up from her glitter sprinkling, but she nods in agreement.

"Like I immediately thought you would be annoying and superficial and have bad taste in music," I say. "I pretty much assessed that in the first second of seeing you again after two years."

"Hey!" shouts Penny, shaking the blue glitter at me.

I watch it sparkle softly in the air, floating onto the table.

"I'm not saying I was right," I say. "Well, except for the music part. Your CDs are awful!"

Penny looks up at me and laughs.

I know I could stop there—that I'm back in my cousin's good graces—but I want to earn that position, so I say what's at the heart of the thing I've been dancing around. "I haven't given you much of a chance to show me who you really are. Penny, you are not a stereotype."

"I'm not?" she asks.

"You have a cross-dressing dog!" I say. "If that isn't defying the norm, I don't know what is."

"I'm just trying to keep Austin weird," Penny says, reciting the slogan that's on every other bumper sticker around this town. She smiles at me.

"You're doing it," I say, "in the best possible way."

"Thanks, Quinn." Penny picks up a bright purple marker and starts drawing the Tri-Pi letters. Then she pauses. "I think you being here makes Austin even weirder. And I know you secretly like *The Bachelor* and are completely in love with Russ."

She laughs like she's kind of kidding as she looks up at me.

I smile at my cousin, and then I feel a tear run down my cheek. It's like when it rains but the sun's still out—completely confusing. I stare hard at the blue glitter, trying to hold in the tears I've been fighting for days now.

"What is it?" asks Penny, reaching out to give me a hug.

And with her arms around me, warm and caring, I let the floodgates go. I start rambling as I snot on her shoulder.

"Sorry," I say, wiping my nose on my sleeve.

"It's okay," says Penny.

She stands up and hands me a tissue from the kitchen island.

"Is this because of that Sebastian guy?" she asks.

"Sort of," I say.

"Did he take advantage of you?" she asks. "Because if he did I will kick his butt from here to Pluto!" She's holding her glue in the air and waving it around like a samurai sword.

"No, no," I say. "Did you see us the other morning? Did it *look* like he was taking advantage?"

"It looked cute," she says, slowing down her glue weaponry display. "You guys were, like, ensnared."

"We were tangled," I say. "And it was just what I wanted. It's like this dream for me because I have the perfect summer fling right in front of me."

"Then why are you crying?" asks Penny.

"I don't know," I say. I'm lying, but I'm also not ready to say it out loud. I do know what's making me feel full of regret. And he lives next door.

After an hour helping Penny with the Rush signs, which I insist need to have some skull stickers and a black outline around the letters' edges, if only to cut the sweetness of Penny's bright pink bubble-heart drawings, I head upstairs and dial Raina.

"Hey," I say.

"Hey!" she says. "Did you get on Facebook to see Eddie yet? What do you think?"

"I haven't been on in a few days," I say. "I just called to apologize."

"Oh," says Raina. "Why?"

"I lied when I said I had to go the other day," I say. "I was feeling this major rush of jealousy."

"Really?" says Raina, sounding fully surprised.

"Yeah," I say. "And I know why. It's because you have the guts to be with a guy you like, even though he's kind of a dork and not what you thought was your Supreme."

"I never had a Supreme, Quinn," says Raina. "That was you, setting your expectations high as always."

"What?" I ask. "Do I do that?"

"Of course!" says Raina. "Remember that time in first grade when you dressed up as a punk? Your mom tried to get you to just put your hair back in a ponytail but you pitched a fit until she figured out how to get it into a perfectly straight, pointy mohawk?"

"Well, spiky hair is pretty much the make-

or-break for that costume," I say, defending my six-year-old self.

Raina laughs. "Yeah, but at the end of the day, did anyone really care whether your hair looked perfect?"

"It's nice if things look perfect," I say.

"And Sebastian does," says Raina. "So what's the issue?"

"Russ," I say, admitting it out loud.

"The cowboy neighbor?!" Raina screams. "Is that dumb frat boy still bothering you?"

"Yeah," I say softly, looking out the window of Miss Tiara's bedroom. Part of me wants to shout at Raina and tell her she sounds really judgmental and narrow-minded. That maybe Russ does have something to offer, and just because he looks all J.Crew catalog doesn't mean he's an empty-minded goon.

"Hey," she says, sounding serious. "Are you upset?"

"I don't know," I say. "I guess I think what you just said about Russ isn't really fair. I mean, he helped me buy a car, he makes really good burgers, and he's trying to show me Austin and new music."

"Whoa—that's the first time I've heard you say something nice about him," says Raina. "You do realize that I've never met him. I'm totally going off of what you've told me."

"And what I've told you is that he's a loser frat boy?" I ask.

"Uh, in short, yeah," she says.

I'm silent as Miss Tiara walks into the room and gives me a cocked-head look like, *What are you doing in my space?* I shoo her out and shut the door. Raina has a point: I have been completely writing Russ off, not to mention talking badly about him.

"I'm sorry," I say. "I'm just really confused."

"It's okay," she says. "But you kind of need to decide who you like. Maybe you shouldn't idealize anyone, Quinn. Follow your instincts. Go for who you really want."

I stare out the window into the parking lot. "But Sebastian is—" I start.

"He's what you *thought* you wanted," she interrupts.

Raina's right. And I think maybe I've been wrong all along.

Chapter 21

I run downstairs and don't even stop to tell Penny where I'm going before I open the sliding glass doors and rush over to Russ and Chrissy's patio. Chrissy's out by the picnic table, cleaning her roller skates.

"Is Russ home?" I ask.

"No," she says, not looking up. "Why?"

"I need to talk to him," I say.

She sighs heavily.

"What?" I ask.

She squints in the sunlight as she gives me a sideways look.

"Quinn, you kinda broke him," she says.

I sink down on the picnic bench across from her.

"Really?" I bite my lip.

"He was, like, devastated when Katie left,"

says Chrissy, looking back down at the skate she's polishing.

"So I heard," I say.

"Yeah, well, he got over it really quickly when he saw you," she says. "It was like someone stuffed a lightning bolt up his butt. The derby girls wanted me to recruit him for our team with the way he was racing around, supercharged."

She looks at me and then smiles, and I can't help but grin.

"But you went for that DJ," she says, smile fading as she refocuses on one particularly stubborn dirt streak near the top of her left skate.

"I didn't think—" I start. But I realize I'm about to say *I didn't think Russ liked me*, and that's not the truth. I guess I didn't think I could like *him*, and when I picture his face with a wide, mocking grin, I can't even remember why. The first time we met I felt electrified. With Sebastian, I was excited because he fit the part. But with Russ, I felt a jolt just because of *him*, of who he was.

"Chrissy, I know I don't deserve your approval," I say. And then I think of a way to appeal to her in her own language. "But I think

Russ and I might be like Mark Darcy and Bridget in *Bridget Jones's Diary*, and all I have to do is just finally tell him that I feel the same way, and then we'll be together and live happily ever after." I can't believe I just cast myself as Bridget Jones.

She looks up at me, and stares hard. Like she's trying to figure out who I am—really. And that makes two of us.

But I also see her eyes start to sparkle slightly. And I know she's giving in.

"He's working on the truck," she says. "You can find him out at Albie's."

"Thank you!" I say, rushing around the table to give her a squeeze.

Then I'm racing back through Penny's condo, grabbing my keys, and, soon, cranking up the Festiva. As I back out of my spot, I reach down absentmindedly to tune the radio, pressing the button to seek through the dial and wishing I hadn't destroyed Russ's mix.

I drive confidently for the first ten minutes, through town and out into the flat plains, which look familiar in their middle-of-nowhere-ness. But after half an hour without hitting Albie's, I think I might be lost. And I haven't seen a gas station or anywhere I can ask for directions in about twenty miles.

I pull the car over to the side of the road and open the glove compartment, hoping against hope that Albie places some magical "free gift with purchase" map in the cars he sells, because I know I sure as H didn't buy one.

I lean over and reach in, but I don't find anything that feels like a map. What I'm touching is a cassette case.

I pull it out and turn it over in my hand.

It's Russ's mix. The one I destroyed. The one I smashed and de-taped and completely annihilated.

I look over the song list, and it's the exact same. But when I peek at the narrow edge of the case to read the title, I see that there's something different. INDIE + COUNTRY, THE RE-MIX, it reads. It's a replacement tape. But how did it get in here?

I hear a knock on my window and I jump.

I turn and see Russ, smirking. I smile back. I've never been so happy to see that pair of mocking dimples.

He moves out of the way and I open my door. When I shut it and turn around to face him, I realize I have no idea what I want to say.

"You lost, Quinn?" he asks.

And the way he says it—*Quinn*—makes me nervous. Like something else is lost, not just me.

"I was trying to find Albie's," I say. "I guess I took a wrong turn."

"Or didn't take the right turn," he says, turning to point down the road. "You missed it about five miles back."

"Oh," I say, feeling silly.

"Is there trouble with the Festiva?" asks Russ. "I'm actually heading out this way to pick up a part for the truck right now, but I can check under your hood if your Sebastian isn't handy with cars."

"No," I say. "I was looking for you, actually."

"For me?" he says. "What for?"

And here it is: My chance to say what I couldn't in the kitchen the other day because I was still tangled up in Sebastian, and I was afraid. I'll tell him that I'm glad I'm the reason he's not with Katie, that I love the things he's shown me in Austin. That I can't get his songs out of my head.

But I'm having trouble voicing the specifics, so I just say, "I'm ready."

Russ tilts his head and looks at me funny. "Ready for what?"

"Ready to go out with you," I say.

And he starts to laugh. At first, it's a quiet chuckle, but it grows into a giant hooting sound, and it's infuriating.

I kick the dust at our feet, and a cloud rises up to interrupt his guffaw-fest. "*What* is so funny?" I ask.

He's holding his stomach, but he gets himself under control for a second.

"The fact that you think it would be that easy," he says. "You had your shot, Miss Priscilla. This bird has flown."

I cross my arms across my chest. "Then why did you leave this replacement mix in my car?" I ask. "Why did you want me to have it so badly that you'd record it again?"

"I can't have you going back to Carolina uneducated," he says. "You need that music, honey. And you need to open your mind. More than anyone I've ever met."

He turns then, and walks back to his truck. He gets in and drives up next to where I'm leaning on the Festiva, a little dumbstruck.

"So your car's running fine?" he asks.

I nod, frowning and refusing to look at his face.

"See you around then, 'Cilla," he says, driving off in a big roar and a mini-cyclone of dust.

I get back into the Festiva and stew for a minute before starting up the engine to turn and go home. *Who the eff does he think he is?*

I have a date with Sebastian tomorrow night, and I might as well keep it. I guess any kind of fling is better than none.

I feel a little bit empty as I drive home, though, and I don't let myself pop in Russ's mix until I'm about halfway there and can't resist any longer.

Chapter 22

The next evening, I hear a honk outside—Sebastian's signature call. *He can't even walk up to the door*, I think.

I step outside and climb on the back of his Vespa, snapping my helmet in place. As we zoom away, I turn back, and I see Russ standing in front of his condo with an arm leaning on the door frame.

He watches us go, and I give him a tiny wave. I'm not even sure he notices it, let alone the feeling behind it. *I wish* . . . but I try to block that thought out of my mind.

We go to this place called the San José. It's a hotel, but there's an outdoor patio where you can sit next to a small swimming pool and order food. The trees provide a pretty, dappled shade, and the people here all look really stylish.

"This is nice," I say, feeling a little under-dressed in my T-shirt and jean shorts, not to mention underage, next to all the sundresses and high heels nearby. There's even a girl from *Project Runway*, I notice, at the table behind us. Not that I watch that show. Very often.

"It's like LA here," says Sebastian.

"Oh," I say, "have you been to LA?"

"No," he says.

I laugh, but he doesn't. I guess Sebastian thinks he can seriously know LA without having been there.

I see Jade walking through the patio. I asked her to come hang out with us. She puts on a good face about the Rick thing, but I know she's been lonely lately.

"Hey, guys," she says, sliding into a seat next to us and flagging down a waiter.

Sebastian orders a fruit-and-cheese plate, which feels fancy and very adult-like. He talks about his latest gig, and Jade and I tell him about the August music festival, which is going to be awesome.

"We'll go to that together," says Sebastian, more telling me than asking me. But I guess I don't mind.

And just when I'm thinking that we're having a nice (if slightly boring) time here, I spot him.

Rick strolls in with some older lady on his arm. Okay, maybe she's like twenty-five, but still. Yuck.

I glance over at Jade to see if she's seen them. She hasn't yet—she's reaching for the last plump red grape. But then she looks up and her eyes widen.

I put my hand on her arm, but I can already see the beginning of major anger working its way across her face.

Sebastian doesn't notice. He's still talking about his upcoming shows and the new samples he's thinking of mixing into his set.

"Just ignore them," I say quietly to Jade, who's watching Rick's and the lady's every move as they sit down at a table across the patio from us. I don't think he's seen us yet.

"Quinn," says Sebastian. "Are you paying attention to me at all?"

"Sorry—Rick just walked in," I say to him.

"Oh, let's go say hi," says Sebastian.

"No!" Jade and I shout simultaneously.

"He and Jade kind of had a . . . falling out," I explain. Sebastian doesn't know anything about the hookup—no one does. Jade and Rick have been okay around each other in the office, but I know seeing him with some woman makes her cat-scratch mad. The look on her face is evidence of that.

"Whoa," says Sebastian, catching Jade's expression. "Must've been a big falling out."

"We hooked up," says Jade. "But it didn't mean anything. To him."

"Rough," says Sebastian. He looks over at Rick and the lady. "You can't blame him though. She's pretty hot."

I glare at Sebastian then, harder than I've glared in a while.

"What?" He shrugs.

"Let's move," says Jade. "I can't watch them all night, but I'm not going to let them chase us out of here either."

The trouble is, the San José patio area is pretty small. We head over by the tiny pool and sit on a couple of deck chairs. There's an old man swimming incredibly short laps in the blue water.

But our movement must draw attention to us, because soon Rick is coming our way.

"Hey there, you guys," he says, like we're a gang of kids he knows or something.

"Hey, man," says Sebastian, standing up to fist-bump Rick.

Jade and I stand too, because it's weird to be down low in a patio chair when Rick's so tall above us.

"Hi," I say.

But Jade doesn't say anything. And when I look over at her, prompting her to *just say hello*, she has this wicked grin on her face.

Before I can stop her, she shoots both arms out, full force, and pushes Rick right into the pool, clothes and all. He misses the lap swimmer by a few inches and the old man gives him a dirty look.

Rick is dumbstruck as he drags his wet head—and shirt and jeans and shoes—out of the pool. He's completely soaked. Have you ever noticed that if you get mad while you're wet, you just look cartoonish? Rick is fuming, which makes him look even sillier.

Jade and I both crack up. I can't help

myself—he looks like a sorry, wet dog, which, if you think about it, isn't a bad metaphor.

"Not cool," says Rick, shaking a dripping finger at Jade as he walks back to his lady-in-waiting. I wish they'd stay so I could hear what's sure to be a *disgruntled intern* explanation, but the lady's already gathering her purse and staring back at us like we're punk kids.

"I think we've officially ditched the grown-up vibe of this place," I say.

Jade laughs some more.

Sebastian, however, is frowning.

"Not cool," he says, echoing Rick.

I look at his brow, furrowed and serious. That lovely mouth that talks only about music and his upcoming sets. Those deep green eyes that drew me in the first time I saw him, but that never seem to really see *me.* That floppy dark hair that probably takes a while to style, even though it's meant to look unkempt and casual. And before I know it, my arms spring out too.

Sebastian, with his tight jeans, his olive-green glasses, and his soft DJ hands, is in the pool.

Jade screams in delight and we both start up again, cackling our heads off. That's when a hotel manager comes over and asks us to leave—all of us.

Outside on the street, Sebastian seems much smaller in his soaking-wet T-shirt, water dripping off his skinny jeans. But it's his angry face that makes me finally see it: He doesn't look like the guy for me at all.

He storms off and hops on his Vespa, not even glancing back at me.

I know it's truly over now. And I think I don't care.

"There's a great country bar right across the street," says Jade.

"Let's go," I say.

And we link arms—dry arms—as we leave our all-wet summer flings behind.

The bar across the street is covered in old wood, and there's a small stage where a really old band is playing classic country tunes. There are middle-aged people twirling around on the dance floor in high-heeled boots and high-waisted jeans (but not the trendy kind). It's amazing.

"I love this," I say, settling onto a wooden stool beside Jade. I realize that if I had come here at the beginning of summer, I would have dismissed the music and the setting. But things are different now.

I sigh out loud, and Jade looks at me sympathetically.

"I'm sure Sebastian will get over it," she says. "He was just mad that he has to go home and restyle his hair."

We both laugh.

"It's not Sebastian," I say. And I look at the couples dancing, thinking back to the night Russ and I spun around to "Can't Help Falling in Love." *Why have I been so stupid?*

"Russ the cowboy," says Jade, following my eyes.

I smile sheepishly at her.

"Remember how you described your dream guy to me at the beginning of the summer?" asks Jade.

"Sort of," I say. "I know Russ doesn't fit that description."

"Actually, I was thinking he does," she says. "You wanted someone who could introduce you to new music, make you playlists, and find songs that you'll always remember from this summer."

"You're right," I say. "He's done all that."

"So what's the issue?" she asks. "Go get your man."

"I tried," I say. "He said no and left me in the dust—literally."

"Really?" asks Jade. "You told him you loved him?"

"Well, not exactly," I say. "I told him I was ready."

She gives me a skeptical look. "Ready for what?" she asks.

"That's what *he* asked," I say. "And I said I was ready to date him."

Jade rolls her eyes. "Gee, Quinn," she says. "You're a regular poet. I can't imagine why a guy wouldn't be swept off his feet when you say those two magical words: 'I'm ready.'"

"Well, he knew what I meant!" I say, frowning.

I slump over on the bar and stare at the carvings in the old wood. JW + ND, DON LOVES TAY, CLEM AND NELL 4-EVER. I pick my head up again. Everywhere I look, people are in love.

"Let me borrow your phone," says Jade.

I reach into my jeans pocket and hand it to

her. No one wants to hear me whine, I guess. I look back up at the band onstage as they finish their set and take a break.

"Penny?" I hear Jade on the phone. "Yeah, Quinn needs you. We're at the Continental Club on South Congress," she says. "Bring Chrissy."

". . . No, nothing life or death," says Jade. "More like a heart intervention."

Through the phone, I hear my cousin's high-pitched scream, which indicates some sort of over-the-top feeling—rage? Excitement? Who can tell? I haven't quite decoded the sorority-shriek sound chart yet.

Jade hangs up and hands my cell back to me.

"Why did you call my cousin?" I ask.

"Reinforcements," she says. "You need a plan to get Russ, and who better to ask for help than two longtime friends of his?"

I smile as Jade tosses her long red hair over one shoulder.

"You have to be willing to do whatever we come up with," says Jade, narrowing her eyes at me. "Even if it's embarrassing."

I nod my head. I've screwed things up

enough on my own—it'll be nice to have a team of love advisors.

"Thanks," I say.

Twenty minutes later, two sorority screams echo in the chill retro bar, and all eyes turn to Chrissy and Penny, who is carrying Miss Tiara in a small brown-and-covered-with-logos purse.

Penny races across the dance floor, weaving in between the befuddled couples to get to us. Chrissy is close behind.

"What did that awful Sebastian do?!" my cousin snaps. "I am going to wring his scrawny little neck when I get ahold of him!"

"It's not Sebastian," I say.

"Yeah," says Jade. "He's kind of . . . um . . . out of the picture now. Right, Quinn?"

I smile as I conjure up the image of the sopping-wet DJ.

"Right," I say.

"What's the deal then?" asks Chrissy. She looks like she might still be mad at me about the Russ stuff.

"Well, obviously you know that Russ completely rejected me the other day," I say.

"Quinn, Russ isn't really a talker," she says. "No, I didn't know. But since Penny told me you were going out with Sebastian tonight, I figured your conversation with him didn't go well."

"I told *you* what happened, right?" I look at Penny. I'm sure I communicated my angst after Russ left me on the road.

"You mean when you came home yesterday and grunted at me before you put your headphones on for the rest of the night?" asks Penny.

Hmm . . . guess I'm not a huge communicator either.

"Okay—so what is the deal?!" asks Penny, waving her hands at me to hurry up and spill it.

I hesitate a minute too long, and Jade is off like a shot. As she recounts the story I told her about me saying "I'm ready," I suddenly realize how dumb and conceited that sounds.

"I'm really smooth," I say sarcastically when Penny and Chrissy smile in pity at my misstep.

"We can fix this," says Penny, going into action mode and taking a purple Sharpie pen out of her bag. Miss Tiara barks in affirmation and the bartender raises an eyebrow. Chrissy flashes a smile (and pushes out her boobs), which makes him back off. Good thing too, because Penny is taking out her Tri-Pi notebook, spreading out across the bar, and starting to write.

WIN HIS HEART: THE RUSS PLAN, she writes.

"What's this?" I ask.

"Just wait," she says. "Now comes the brainstorming. You didn't know your old cousin was a boy genius."

"You're a hyper-smart eleven-year-old boy?" asks Jade.

"I mean a genius with guys," says Penny, waving off Jade's joke. "Now let's get going."

Penny makes us write down romantic ideas — poetry, flowers, music, dancing—and under each column, we have to come up with specifics that Russ likes. So Chrissy chimes in and tells us that he used to have a thing for Edgar Allan Poe, while I note that he mentioned bluebonnets once and that we've danced to "Can't Help Falling in Love."

"But his favorite song is that 'Waltz Across Texas' one," says Chrissy. "He hums it constantly."

I grin.

Then Penny adds "Sports" because she says that—to guys—that is romantic. And Chrissy suggests that I wear a UT cheerleading uniform while I carry out the activities (that's the third part of the brainstorming session). Jade nixes that part so I don't have to. *Phew.*

By the time we finish, five pages of the notebook are covered with doodles and dreams of romance, and I have a plan.

"Are you ready?" asks Jade.

"Have I not made it clear by now that I am?" I joke.

"Took you long enough!" says Chrissy, smiling.

Penny, Chrissy, and Jade reach in for a group hug, and suddenly I'm feeling like, no matter what Russ says, this is the Best. Summer. Ever.

Chapter 23

After calling about ten florists, I realize that bluebonnets are hard to come by in July. As one lady put it, "That's a spring flower, hon. How about a nice boo-kay of Knock Out roses?" So that's what I got, and it turns out that Knock Out is their official name—they're hearty, which seems suiting for Russ. They're also pink, but hey, that made Penny happy.

So I tie those up with a bow and include a little card that says, YOUR NEXT CLUE IS AT THE BADDEST-ASS FLAG EVER.

He'll find my second message stuck into the corner of the case by the "Come and Take It" flag in the Four Seasons hotel lobby. That note says, SUPPER'S ON ME—THE BEST BBQ IN TOWN, OR SO YOU SAY.

He'll take off for Iron Works, where I have

an order in for a plate of barbecue and a big pickle, along with slaw and hush puppies on the side, of course. On his tray, the owner promised to deliver note number three.

That one's the scariest. It'll direct Russ to the Continental Club, where Chrissy and Penny managed to convince the band that was playing on our night of plotting to do a very, very big favor for us. All in the name of summer love.

I'm standing in the corner of the Continental, staring at the clock. It's getting close to eight P.M., which is the ETA for Russ. The plan was that he got the Knock Out roses at around six P.M., when Chrissy would pretend she heard the doorbell and they'd be lying on the welcome mat outside as Russ went to check it. She texted me a little after six, and the text just said, **Russter is on the move.**

So he must've gotten to the Four Seasons by six-thirty or so, where Jade was waiting in dark glasses and a hat, lingering near the flag to be sure Russ found clue number two. Her text, sent at 6:42 said, **The rooster has picked up his hen.**

Funny how this clue game is making everyone

into weird code-talkers. That one made me laugh.

Iron Works Barbecue is nearby, and Penny would be there, pretending to bump into Russ. Even though I hadn't gotten a text from her by seven, I headed to the bar to wait. But now it's close to eight, and she still hasn't—

beepbeepbeep

Penny: **He's on his way.**

Phew. And no code talk. But then a second text comes in.

Penny: **He says it's all or nothing.**

I have no idea what that means, but I can feel my heart beating in my throat as I wave at Tom the bartender.

"Ready?" he asks.

"Ten minutes," I say. And I try to sound confident, but my voice shakes a little.

Tom signals to the band, making a "10" with both hands. The lead singer, an older man with a white beard and a rough but perfect voice whom Tom calls "Pick-up Pete," nods as they finish up their song.

I lean back on the bar, glad I had my friends make sure Russ took each step of the bait. I also wanted them to supervise the earlier parts of this plan because I don't want them at Location Four—here. I made them promise that they'd let Russ come alone. This is a one-time humiliation for a good cause. My heart. But I don't want too many witnesses. Especially not a family member who can tell the story for ages.

Pick-up Pete finishes one more song, and then announces that the band will take a quick break. He steps down off the stage, walking over to me.

"You the singing girl?" he asks.

"Yeah," I say, still not sounding very solid.

"And you know the words to this song," he says, looking me up and down like he's not so sure that a blue-haired girl wearing a Walters T-shirt and Converse sneaks can pull off the country classic we have lined up.

"I do," I say. It's all I've listened to for the past three days as Penny and Chrissy and Jade helped me get the clues ready and this final moment set up.

"Well, then, where's the fella?" asks Pick-up Pete.

As if on cue, Russ walks in. Followed by Chrissy, Jade, and Penny.

I glance down at my phone and reread the second text from my cousin. That's what she meant by "all or nothing"—he wouldn't come without them. Russ is getting his way *again* by bringing everyone here! And I start to fume, but then I look up at them, and I catch Russ's eye. His smile grows a few inches, and I see he's holding the flowers.

"I'm ready," I say to Pick-up Pete. Then I take his arm and let him walk me up the steps to the stage.

I shake hands with the band members, who eye me with kindness. Or is it pity?

I don't have time to think too much, because Pick-up Pete is already at the mike.

"Ladies and Gents, we have a special treat tonight," he says. "We're going to perform an Ernest Tubbs classic with a very special song-bird."

He winks at me and I smile. I try to look out in the audience, but there are stage lights in my eyes, so I can't see where Russ is.

"Miss Quinn Parker would like to—" he starts.

I tap him on the shoulder, interrupting, and

I whisper in his ear.

"Excuse me," he continues. "Miss *Priscilla* Quinn Parker would like to dedicate this song to one Mr. Russ Jay Barnes, who is the most amazing effing frat boy she's ever met."

I hear laughter and a few hoots from the audience then, and the encouraging sounds buoy me to the mike.

The band strikes up a slow beat, and I come in right on cue.

"When we dance together, my world's in disguise . . .

"It's a fairyland tale that's come true . . ."

My voice isn't entirely melodic. Okay, it's pretty awful. I'm not even on key. But I keep going, warbling about the stars in his eyes, how he takes away my heartaches and troubles. This is a song that I hadn't even heard until Russ made it the closing song on his mix, but I am completely taken with it. Maybe it's that feeling that's carrying me through this paltry vocal performance. When I end with "I could waltz across Texas with you . . ." I feel a tear run down my cheek.

I hear the bar patrons clapping politely, probably not sure what to make of the subpar "songbird," as Pick-up Pete called me. But then I hear the applause growing. It's getting louder and louder and I hold my hand out in front of my face to block the spotlights so I can see what's going on.

Just then, I feel the wind under me as Russ lifts me up in his arms, twirling me around once and then setting me down, back on the stage. I don't even care that there are two dozen people watching—including my cousin. I lean in to meet Russ's amazing lips. And we have the best freaking kiss this stage has ever seen.

When my eyes and ears refocus as we part, I hear more cheers and hoots, and I suddenly remember to be a little embarrassed. I give a shy wave as Russ leads me down the stage stairs.

I don't even say good-bye to Penny or Jade or Chrissy as he pulls my hand and we dash outside.

"Leave your car," he says.

My cheeks flush again as I hop into his truck, more lovestruck than I ever knew I could be.

Epilogue

I've had three weeks with Russ by my side. As I wake up next to him in his double bed, where I've been sleeping pretty regularly, I realize that this is the second half of the last weekend of the last week of our summer. I fly home tomorrow. I'll see Raina and my parents, and I'll make trips to Target to buy things like a laundry basket and storage bins and folding bookshelves for my college dorm room. I leave in just two more weeks for Vermont.

I look at Russ, sleeping, and my heart starts to sink a little.

But then he opens his eyes.

"Good morning, sunshine," he says, wrapping me up in his arms for five more minutes in bed.

I look up at the ceiling, where a poster of some

famous UT quarterback is taped above the bed. The walls are covered in party photos — mostly from frat keggers — and there are wooden Alpha-Alpha letters hanging on back of the door.

If I'd had a crystal ball three months ago, just before I came to Austin, and I'd been able to see where I'd end up hanging out — in this room, with this guy — I would have been mortified. Because back then, I had all these ideas about who I was, and who my friends were supposed to be, and who I didn't want to know.

I lean over and kiss Russ on the cheek. With the help of Penny and Chrissy — and Jade, too — I have so much more now.

The Amalgam festival went amazingly well — after Rick dried off he was able to laugh at the getting-thrown-in-pool incident. He even gave both me and Jade small stipends for our summer work, which will help with college stuff next year. He also gave Jade something more important — the full-on "I'm a dick" apology. It even sounded sincere.

Jade's response was awesome. "That was so three weeks ago," she said. "I'm over it."

I half expected Sebastian to call me or stop

by Amalgam after the San José pool incident, but he stayed away that whole next week. I was busy with Russ, mostly, but I felt like I had to say something to him, so I stopped by Dirty's the next Friday night when he was deejaying.

I walked in and saw that he was taking a break, in a booth, with his arm around some other girl, who looked way more indie than I do. Black hair, cat's eye glasses, patchwork dress. She was straight outta Hipster-land. My jealous instinct didn't kick in even a little bit, and I went over and talked to him like nothing had happened. He acted the same way. And when I left, I smiled and waved one last time, happy that he found someone he wanted, too. Or at least the possibility of someone.

I muss Russ's hair and climb out of bed. I go downstairs and walk out the back door, heading to Penny's kitchen to grab an apple. She's sitting at the island bar with Miss Tiara in her robe. That is, both of them are in robes.

"Morning," I say.

"Hola, Juliet," she says. "Last night with Romeo tonight?"

"Yeah," I say, not wanting to think of it that way.

"What are you guys doing?" she asks. And it seems like maybe she's wondering if we're going to hole up in Russ's room and not hang out. Which is so not our style.

"Something with you," I say.

That night, Miss Tiara, Penny, Chrissy, Jade, Russ, and I stake out a spot on the lawn of the Four Seasons Hotel around six P.M. We spread a big blanket over the grass and order frothy root beers, looking toward the sky and hoping we'll see something special.

Namely, bats.

"I'm telling you, they're flying tonight," says Russ. "I can feel it."

"I read on some website that they fly on warm, calm evenings—sometimes even *before* sunset," says Jade.

The six of us talk about plans for next year. Penny, Chrissy, and Russ will all be UT seniors; Jade is starting college in Dallas. And I'll be in Vermont, which I'm sure will feel worlds away from here.

I look down at the blanket for a minute, getting sad.

Russ picks up my chin. "Take a quick walk with me?" he asks, grabbing the backpack he brought and reaching out for my hand.

"Sure," I say. "We'll be right back, guys."

"Take your tiiiime," says Chrissy while Penny makes a kissy face. *Sorority girls, man.*

We walk down to the edge of the river, heading away from the bridge a little bit so we're out of the Tri-Pi-Jade sight range.

Russ unzips his bag and hands me a bouquet of tiny, blue, star-shaped flowers.

"They're forget-me-nots," he says. And I can see him blushing.

"Subtle, Russ." I laugh and he reaches down to pick me up and spin me around, which is my new favorite move ever. I don't think anyone else will ever do it as well as he does.

"So are we gonna have the breakup talk now?" I ask. "Because I don't really want to voice it, you know? Can't we just say good-bye and not know what it means?"

"I'm not giving up," says Russ. "I've got too much to lose."

I smile at him indulgently. I know college will be a whole new world, just like this summer. I can't promise him anything.

"Priscilla," he starts, using his Elvis voice so things don't get too mushy. "I'm a practical guy. And I have a practical plan."

"Oh, really?" I ask. "What's that?"

He reaches back into his bag and hands me a card. On the front are two crudely drawn shapes—one in blue that is small and long, one in orange that's rounder and much bigger. There's a green X in between them.

"Hieroglyphics?" I ask.

"States!" he says, pointing at the smaller, longer one. "That's North Carolina."

"Um . . . okay," I say. "And this one is . . ."

"Texas!"

"Aha," I say. "So this is you and me . . ."

"Right," he says. "South by Southwest."

I open the card and read the inside:

Meet me in Austin, by the Walters stage.
Love, Russ

"I don't get it," I say, wishing I did.

"The music festival next spring!" he shouts.

"I know what South by Southwest is!" I say, getting annoyed. He can still frustrate me faster than any guy I've ever met. But I'm smiling too. "What does it mean?" I ask.

"No obligations," he says. "But if you can't get me out of your mind, and if I can't get you out of mine, here's where and when our next date will happen."

I look down at the card again, and it starts to make sense. In a completely impractical way, but also in a romantic one.

"I'll be there," I say, not knowing whether I'll be able to keep my word, but knowing that I mean it in this moment, and that's all that matters.

And then, we hear a collective "Ooooohhh" rising from the lawn.

I look up and see a stream of black bats flowing out from under the Congress Avenue Bridge. Their fast-beating wings make a sound like a rhythm section, and they're so close together that it looks like the golden-pink horizon is being covered in black velvet. Russ grabs my hand and we run back to join Penny,

Jade, and Chrissy.

The five of us stand together, Penny holding Miss Tiara, as the bats blanket the sky, covering Austin with the magic of an unexpected journey.